"Don't you trust me?"

"I trust you." She swallowed, and rubbed one hand, palm down, along the side of her thigh. "But I'm not sure I trust myself."

"What do you mean?" He tried to read her expression, but she wasn't giving off clear signals. Was she afraid? Angry? Guilty?

"I'm not the person you think I am," she said.

"How do you know what I think about you?"

"It's what everyone thinks about me—that I'm this quiet, plain, serious woman who never steps out of line. I'm responsible and sober and dependable and I never cause any trouble at all."

"Are you saying you have caused trouble?" he asked.

"More than you can imagine."

COLORADO BODYGUARD

CINDI MYERS

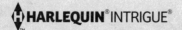

For Denise

Recycling programs
for this product may
not exist in your area.

ISBN-13: 978-0-373-74907-2

Colorado Bodyguard

Printed in U.S.A.

www.Harlequin.com

Cindi Myers is an author of more than fifty novels. When she's not crafting new romance plots, she enjoys skiing, gardening, cooking, crafting and daydreaming. A lover of small-town life, she lives with her husband and two spoiled dogs in the Colorado mountains.

Books by Cindi Myers

The Ranger Brigade

The Guardian
Lawman Protection
Colorado Bodyguard

Harlequin Intrigue

Rocky Mountain Revenge
Rocky Mountain Rescue

Harlequin Heartwarming

Her Cowboy Soldier
What She'd Do for Love

Visit the Author Profile page at Harlequin.com for more titles.

CAST OF CHARACTERS

Randall "Rand" Knightbridge—The Bureau of Land Management officer joined The Ranger Brigade task force to help fight crime on public lands. He prefers working outdoors and the company of his police dog, Lotte, to the company of most other people.

Sophie Montgomery—The quiet, reserved woman has traveled from Wisconsin to search for her missing sister in the wilderness of Colorado. She's always lived in Lauren's shadow, and has begun to question the sacrifices she's made for her sister.

Lauren Starling—The popular prime-time anchor for a Denver news channel has been missing a month, since her car was found abandoned at an overlook in Black Canyon of the Gunnison National Park. With no evidence of foul play and rumors that Lauren suffered from depression in the wake of a divorce and trouble on the job, the Rangers fear she may have come to the park to commit suicide.

The Ranger Brigade—An interagency task force of law enforcement officers charged with fighting crime on public lands in Southwest Colorado, including Black Canyon of the Gunnison National Park, Curecanti Wilderness Area and Gunnison Gorge Wilderness Area.

Richard Prentice—The infamous billionaire has made a career out of manipulating state and federal government officials, but The Ranger Brigade refuses to bend to his will. Is Prentice the power behind the recent crime wave, or are his criticisms of the Rangers justified?

Phil Starling—The down-on-his-luck actor has relied on support payments from his ex-wife, Lauren. As the beneficiary of her million-dollar life insurance policy, he has plenty of reasons for wanting her dead.

Alan Milbanks—The owner of a local fish shop met with Lauren shortly before she disappeared. Did she discover that fish aren't the only thing Alan has been dealing from his storefront?

Lotte—Rand's Belgian Malinois. The dog is both his working partner and his best friend.

Graham Ellison—Captain of The Ranger Brigade.

Emma Wade—The reporter has devoted her career to seeking justice for crime victims. Author of a profile of billionaire Richard Prentice, she knows more about him than almost anyone. She's engaged to Graham Ellison.

Chapter One

The canyon tore a deep gash in the open landscape. Sheer rock walls plunged to a river that was invisible below, lost in blackness. Darker red and gray rock painted the chasm walls in fanciful shapes that resembled two warring Chinese dragons, engaged in a battle that had been going on for centuries.

Sophie Montgomery stood at the edge of the overlook, fighting waves of vertigo as she tried to peer down into the canyon's depths. She struggled to imagine her sister, Lauren, standing in this same, desolate spot. Lauren had battled plenty of demons in her life; which one had brought her to this lonely, forbidding place?

Lauren, where are you? Sophie sent the silent plea across the canyon, but only wind and the distant hum of traffic answered.

She shivered again, despite the summer heat, and turned away from the overlook and headed back to her car, walking past an RV and a mom and two children posing in front of the canyon while Dad snapped the picture. They all looked thrilled to be here, though Sophie had never understood the attraction of a camping vacation. She and Lauren had always agreed that getaways should involve nice hotels, preferably with swimming pools and room service. One more reason it didn't make sense that Lauren had come to what must be one of the most remote spots in her adopted home state.

Sophie slid back behind the wheel of her rental car and jammed the key into the ignition. She didn't want to be here, but then, she hadn't especially wanted to be any of the other places that looking out for Lauren had taken her over the years. The only difference was that this time felt scarier. More hopeless. Lauren had done some crazy, wild things over the years, but she'd never stayed gone this long before. And she'd never been in a place where Sophie couldn't reach her. Sometimes, when Lauren was going through a really bad spell, Sophie was the only one who *could* reach her.

She backed out of her parking space and turned the car around, headed toward the park entrance. The police in Denver had been kind— sympathetic, even. But they had found no evidence that Lauren had been abducted, and given her recent history, they suspected she'd run away—or worse. "We understand your sister struggled with depression," the detective who had spoken to her said.

"She was handling it," Sophie had told him. "She was under a doctor's care."

His look was full of sympathy and little hope.

She checked the time on her phone. Five minutes until her appointment with a member of the special task force assigned to deal with crimes in the area. This time, she'd be more assertive. She would make the officer understand that Lauren wouldn't have run away. And she wouldn't have taken her own life. She was in trouble and they had to help.

Lauren had no one else to speak for her; it was up to Sophie to look after her little sister, just as she'd always done.

She turned the car into the gravel lot in front of the portable building that served as headquarters for The Ranger Brigade—the interagency task force focused on fighting crime on public lands in western Colorado. A hot wind blasted her as she exited the car, whipping her shoulder-length brown hair into her eyes and sending a tumbleweed bobbing across her path. She stared at the beach-ball-sized sphere of dried weeds as it bounced across the pavement and into the brush across the road. The whole scene was like something out of a Wild West movie, as foreign from her life back in Madison, Wisconsin, as she could imagine.

As she made her way up a gravel walkway toward the building, a large dog—blond with a black muzzle and tail, like a German shepherd, but smaller—loped from around the side of the building. Sophie froze, heart pounding, struggling to breathe. The dog kept running toward her, tongue lolling, teeth glinting in the bright sun. She closed her eyes, fighting wave after wave of paralyzing fear.

"Lotte! Down!"

Sophie opened her eyes to see the dog immediately stop and lie down. A young man trotted around the side of the building. Tall and muscular, with closely cropped brown hair, he wore tan trousers and a tan long-sleeved shirt. "Don't worry, she's harmless," he called.

Sophie shifted her attention back to the dog, reminding herself to breathe. The dog grinned up at her, tongue hanging out. To most people she probably did look harmless. But Sophie wasn't most people.

"Can I help you?" the man asked as he drew closer. Green eyes studied her, fine lines fanning from the corners, though she had a sense that he wasn't much older than her own thirty. The buffeting wind and too-bright sun didn't seem to bother him. In fact, he looked right at home against the backdrop of cactus and stunted pinion. He could have been an old-west lawman, with a silver star pinned to his chest, or a cowboy, ready to ride the range—any of those strong, romantic archetypes with the power to make a woman swoon.

Except she hadn't come here to ogle the local stud lawman, she reminded herself. Even if guys like him paid any attention to quiet bookworms like her. "I'm Sophie Montgomery. I have an appointment with the Rangers," she said.

"Right. Officer Rand Knightbridge." He offered his hand. "Come on in and we'll get started."

She took his hand, but released it quickly, focused on the dog who sat quietly at his side. It was a powerful animal, its eyes alert, as if at any moment it might lunge. "I'm afraid of dogs," she said, and took a step back.

He stopped and looked from her to the dog. "Lotte is very well trained," he said. "She won't hurt you, I promise."

"I didn't say it was a rational fear, I said I was afraid." Why did people always want to argue with her about this? No one ever tried to understand.

"Sure. I'll put her inside, in another room."

"All right. I'll wait out here."

He glanced at her again, then turned and snapped his fingers. "Lotte! Come!"

The dog fell into step beside him, gazing up at him adoringly.

She crossed her arms over her chest and tried not to feel self-conscious. The windows on the Rangers' headquarters were covered by blinds, but she had a feeling she was being watched. She fought the urge to stick her tongue out at whoever was looking, but that compulsion died when she reminded herself why she was here. She needed for these people to take her concerns seriously.

After a moment, during which she gave up trying to keep the wind from whipping her hair into her eyes, the front door to the trailer opened and Officer Knightbridge waved to her. "The coast is clear," he said. "It's safe to come in."

She made her way up the walkway and through the door he held open for her. The office itself was Spartan and utilitarian, with industrial carpet and simple furnishings. "Let's use the conference room, back here," Knightbridge said, leading her to another open doorway.

A woman at a computer looked up and smiled at her as they passed and two other uniformed officers glanced her way but didn't acknowledge her. In the conference room, Officer Knightbridge pulled out a folding chair at the scarred table, then took a similar chair across from her.

"How can I help you, Ms. Montgomery?" he asked.

"My sister, Lauren Starling, has been missing since May twenty-eighth. That's when she left for a week's vacation, but no one's seen or heard from her since. The Denver Police Department suggested I contact you to see how the investigation into her disappearance is progressing."

There was a flicker of confusion in his green eyes. He shifted in his seat. "The Denver Police Department told you we were investigating your sister's disappearance."

"I understand her car was found abandoned very near here."

"Yes, I believe it was."

"And your organization deals with crime in the park?"

"The park and surrounding public lands."

"So, naturally, I assumed you're investigating my sister's disappearance."

As she'd talked, the lines on his forehead had deepened. The metal folding chair squeaked as he shifted position again. "Ms. Montgomery…"

"Please, call me Sophie." She wanted him to trust her, to confide in her, even.

"Ms. Montgomery, a car registered to your sister was found at the Dragon Point overlook in the park. There were no signs of violence, no notes and nothing else that pointed to violence.

Park rangers conducted a search for your sister and found nothing. They had the car towed to an impound lot and contacted Denver police, and they also notified us to be on the lookout for her."

"I know all that," she said, trying to quell her impatience. "That's why I'm here. I want to know what you've discovered since then."

His expression grew even more pained. "After you called, I reviewed what little information we have. No one has seen or heard from your sister. The Denver police led us to believe your sister had come here of her own free will."

"She may have come here voluntarily, but she didn't just walk away from her car, her home, her job, her friends and her family." Sophie fought to keep the agitation from her voice. "Something has happened to her."

"The report I read said that your sister has a history of depression."

Here it was, the excuse they all gave for not taking Lauren's disappearance more seriously. "She's recently been diagnosed with bipolar disorder—what people used to call manic depression. She was in treatment, on medication and doing well."

"The report we received said she was recently divorced."

"Yes." Lauren had adored Phil; she'd been

crushed when he announced he'd fallen in love with a woman he worked with. She'd had to cope not only with the end of her marriage, but also with the humiliation of his very public infidelity. But she was rallying. "My sister is much stronger than people give her credit for," Sophie said. "I talked to her only two days before she disappeared and she was very upbeat, excited about a new project at work."

"The police report also said she'd been put on probation at the TV station—that she was in danger of losing her job."

"She told me she wasn't worried about that—that this new project would prove how valuable she was."

This seemed to spark some interest in him. "Did she say what the project was?"

"No. She didn't like to talk about things like that until after they were complete. She was superstitious that way."

The frown returned. "Ms. Montgomery... Sophie." He leaned toward her, elbows on the table, hands loosely clasped. "Do you know the number one reason automobiles are abandoned within the park?"

"No." But clearly he was going to tell her. And the expression in his eyes told her she wouldn't like what she heard.

"For whatever reason, national parks are popular places for people to take their own lives. The canyon seems to offer what some perceive as an easy way out. If they don't drive right off the cliff, they park the car and jump. When a Ranger sees a car parked in the same place for days, he knows he may be looking at a possible suicide. And when the missing person is known to have been depressed…" He spread his hands wide, allowing her to fill in the rest of the thought.

But she refused to go there. "So you're telling me you haven't even investigated my sister's disappearance? She's been missing a month and no one is looking for her?"

"You need to prepare yourself." He sat back in his chair, his face calm, eyes still locked to hers. "There's a good chance your sister is no longer alive."

RAND HAD PUT his assessment of her sister's situation as delicately as he knew how, but he could see by the pain and anger in Sophie Montgomery's brown eyes that he'd been too blunt. Despite all the evidence pointing to this conclusion, she didn't believe her sister had committed suicide. Without a body she'd never believe, and unfortunately, the vastness and remoteness of the parklands made finding a body difficult—

sometimes impossible. "I'm sorry," he said. "I wish I had better news for you."

And he wished he had more time for her. So much of his job involved dealing with the dregs of society—drug dealers and killers and people who preyed on the innocent. It was nice to sit with a pretty woman who dressed well and had a soft voice and manicured hands, and just talk.

If only their topic of conversation had been more pleasant. And if only he had more time to listen to her soft, educated voice. But everyone on the task force was under pressure to root out the criminals who'd turned a sleepy corner of Colorado into a center for drug dealing, human trafficking and all manner of violent crime. They'd made some arrests and succeeded in slowing the flow of drugs and illegal aliens, but they'd yet to find the person or persons overseeing the whole operation. They were certain someone was in charge, and had ideas about who that might be, but still lacked the evidence they needed.

Meanwhile, perpetual thorn in their side Richard Prentice, a billionaire who'd made a name for himself causing trouble for local, state and federal authorities, continued to harangue about the need to disband the task force altogether. He filed lawsuits claiming the officers harassed him, held press conferences to point out how much taxpayers spent to fund the Rangers and how little they received in return. And all the while, he sat in his mansion on private land adjacent to the park, protected by his money and a team of lawyers. As far as Rand was concerned, Richard Prentice was suspect number one when it came to crime in the area, but as his boss, Captain Graham Ellison, so often reminded him, being a jerk didn't make a man guilty.

And being a jerk wasn't winning Rand any points with Sophie Montgomery. "My sister did not commit suicide," she said. "I don't care how many times you or the police in Denver or anyone else tell me so. I know her better than anyone, and she wouldn't have done that." She opened her purse and took out a small spiral notebook. "I came here today to convince you that Lauren is worth looking for. The least you can do is hear me out."

Her eyes, full of so much determination…and not a little fear, met his. In that moment, he saw all it had taken for her to come here, knowing that pursuing her quest might only lead to the end of all hope for her sister. Her courage moved him, and fueled his growing attraction to this quiet, determined woman. "Of course," he said. "I'll be happy to listen to what you have to say. Would you mind if I brought in my commander and some other officers, as well?"

"No, not at all." Her lower lip trembled, but she quickly brought it under control. "Thank you."

He resisted the urge to cover her hand with his own; she might take his gesture of comfort the wrong way. He left the conference room, shutting the door behind him, and found Graham in his office. "Lauren Starling's sister is here," he said. "She doesn't think Lauren ran away or killed herself. She thinks she might be in real trouble."

Graham, a big man with the imposing demeanor of the US Marine he had once been, looked up from a stack of files. "Does she have any information that would help us find her sister?" he asked.

"I don't know, but I thought we should hear her out."

"All right. Who else is here?"

"Carmen and Simon were in the computer room a little while ago. And Marco is around somewhere."

"Then round them up and ask them to report to the conference room. Maybe one of us will spot something in the sister's story that will help."

Ten minutes later, they all converged on the conference room. Sophie shrank a little as they crowded into the room—a mass of brown uniforms, all male except for Colorado Bureau of Investigations officer Carmen Redhorse. Carmen sat on one side of Sophie. Rand sat across from her; he wanted to be able to see her expressive face as she talked. He often learned more about people from their body language and emotions than their words.

"Ms. Montgomery, I'm Captain Graham Ellison. These are officers Simon Woolridge, Carmen Redhorse and Marco Cruz. I understand you have some information to share with us about your sister, Lauren Starling."

"Yes." She glanced at Rand and he nodded encouragingly. She looked down at her notebook. "I spoke with my sister on May twenty-sixth, and she was very upbeat, excited about a new project she was working on—one she said would prove to the television station that she was too valuable to let go. She'd been to see her doctor recently and she said she was doing really well on her medication. She had been through some hard things recently, but she was looking forward to the future. She wasn't a woman who was despondent, or who wanted to take her life."

"What kind of medication?" Graham asked.

Sophie's face flushed, but she kept her chin up, and met the captain's direct gaze. "About six months ago, Lauren was diagnosed with bipolar disorder. She'd struggled for years, primarily with mania. The stress of the divorce and job pressures made it worse and there had been a couple of…episodes that forced her to take some time off work. But with the proper diagnosis and treatment, she'd been doing much better. And as I said, she was very excited about this project."

"What was the project?" Carmen asked.

"I don't know. But something to do with work, I think."

"She was the prime-time news anchor at Channel Nine in Denver?" Simon, an agent with Immigration and Customs Enforcement, asked.

"Yes. And as I believe you've already learned, she had been told her job was in jeopardy."

"Why was that?" Graham asked.

The worried furrow in her forehead deepened. "She wouldn't say outright, and the station refused to talk to me, but I suspect it was because of her sometimes erratic behavior in the months prior to her diagnosis as bipolar. She missed some work and showed up other times unprepared. But she was doing much better in the weeks before she disappeared. She was happy to know what was going on and was following her doctor's orders and feeling better."

"But that didn't stop the station from threatening to let her go?" Carmen said.

"Ratings had fallen. Lauren told me she was going to do something that would boost ratings."

"Maybe she came here to hide." Marco Cruz, with the DEA, spoke so quietly Rand wasn't sure he'd heard him correctly at first.

"Hide?" Sophie asked. "From what?"

"Maybe she faked her disappearance to draw attention to herself and to the station, and then she planned to emerge after a few weeks in the headlines." Marco shrugged. "People have faked all kinds of things for attention, from gunshot wounds and muggings to their own deaths."

"Lauren isn't faking anything," Sophie said. "She started her career as an investigative reporter. I think she had a lead on a big crime and came here to report on it."

"What kind of crime?" Graham shifted in his chair, the only sign that he was growing impatient.

"I don't know. It would have to be something big, if she was going to boost ratings."

"And she didn't tell you anything?" Carmen spoke slowly, thoughtfully.

"No—just that she was working on a new project that would fix everything."

"And she never said anything about coming to Montrose or Black Canyon Park or anything like that?" Simon snapped off the question, as if interrogating a suspect. Rand knew this was just his way, but Sophie bridled at this approach.

"No," she said, and pressed her lips together, clamming up.

"How often did you talk to her?" Rand asked.

She turned toward him. "Once a week or so. Sometimes more often."

"Anyone else she was close to? A best friend? Neighbors?"

"She still talked to her ex-husband, Phil, occasionally. Have you interviewed him?"

Rand frowned. "Why do you think we should talk to him?"

"Aren't husbands—or ex-husbands—always the first people police suspect when someone disappears?"

"It depends on the case," Graham said. "Did Lauren and Phil Starling have a contentious relationship?"

She flushed. "No. I mean, she wasn't happy about the divorce—he was cheating on her, after all. And he left her to be with the other woman."

"But she'd already granted the divorce, right?" Simon asked. "She didn't put any obstacles in his way."

"No. She even agreed to pay support, since she made more money than he did."

"So he didn't really have any reason to follow her from Denver to Montrose and do her harm," Rand said.

"We don't know that for sure. And you won't

know until you talk to him." She looked stubborn, chin up, mouth set in a firm line.

"What about other family members?" he asked. "Brothers, sisters, parents?"

She shook her head. "There's just the two of us. Our parents were killed in a car accident when I was a sophomore in college. Lauren was a senior in high school."

"So you're used to looking after her," he said.

"Yes."

"Maybe she resented that," Simon said. "Maybe she purposely kept things from you."

"I'm sure she kept a great deal from me. Whatever you think, I didn't try to run her life. But I know her. She wouldn't take her own life. And you can quote statistics all day long, but even if—and it's a huge *if* in my mind—even if she wanted to kill herself, why would she travel five hours away from her home to disappear in a national park?"

"Sometimes people choose a place that's meaningful to them," Marco said. "One they associate with memories or special people."

"She'd never been here before. This park meant nothing special to her. She loved the city. She wasn't a hiker or a camper or anything like that."

"So why was she here?" Graham brought

them back to the essential question. "What was this story you think she was working on?"

"I don't know, but it must have been something major, if she thought it could save her career."

"If she wanted to report on a major crime, you'd think she'd stay in Denver," Carmen said.

"Except you guys are here." Sophie sat up straighter, and looked them each in the eye. "Why form a special task force if there isn't something big going on here? I did my homework. I know about the drug busts, the human-trafficking ring and the murder of that pilot. Maybe Lauren had uncovered something to do with all that."

"She never came to us, or to local law enforcement with that information," Graham said.

"Maybe she never had time," Sophie said.

"In the course of your research, did you see the newspaper articles about your sister's disappearance?" Graham asked. "Written by a local reporter who's taken an interest in the story."

"Emma Wade. Yes, I read the stories. I plan to talk to her, but I came to you first."

Rand watched the captain closely. Only those who knew him well would register the slight flush that reddened the tips of his ears at the mention of reporter Emma Wade—soon to be

Emma Ellison. Her reporting on Lauren Starling's disappearance had put her at odds with the gruff commander at first, but now they were engaged.

"Ms. Wade came to us with her concerns about your sister and we have followed every lead," Graham said. "But there's nothing there." He slid back his chair and stood. "I'm sorry, Ms. Montgomery, I wish I had better news for you. If you find out something more, don't hesitate to contact us."

The others started moving chairs and rising also. Carmen gave Sophie a sympathetic look and patted her shoulder. Sophie's expression clouded and Rand braced himself for a storm— of tears or anger, he wasn't sure which.

But she was stronger—and more determined— than he'd given her credit for. "Wait," she said. "There's one other thing that might tie her to this area—to your jurisdiction."

Graham paused on his way to the door. "What's that?"

She dug in her purse and held up a small rectangle of white cardboard. "I found this in her apartment. It was tucked into a book beside the bed—the police said they searched her apartment, but they obviously didn't feel this was significant."

Randall took the piece of thin cardboard and stared at the crisp black letters on its glossy finish.

"What is it?" Simon demanded.

"It's a business card." He turned it over and over, then looked up at his coworkers. "A business card for Richard Prentice."

Chapter Two

Sophie tried to read the look that passed between the officers. The business card definitely interested them. "Do you know Richard Prentice?" she asked. "Have you asked him if he knows anything about my sister's disappearance?"

"You don't know Prentice?" Rand Knightbridge asked. "Your sister didn't mention him?"

"She never said anything about him. And I'm not from here, so I don't keep up with local people and events. I looked him up on the internet, but all I learned is that he's a very rich businessman and he has an estate near the park. That seems significant, don't you think? Maybe she came here to see him."

"Where are you from?" Captain Ellison asked.

"Madison, Wisconsin. Tell me about Richard Prentice."

"Like you said, he's a rich guy who owns a mansion near here," Officer Woolridge said, his sour expression making clear his opinion of Prentice.

"We should talk to him," Sophie said. "Maybe he knows why Lauren was here. Maybe she interviewed him for a story."

Again, Rand and the captain exchanged looks. "What is it?" she demanded. "What aren't you telling me?"

"Prentice is an agitator," Woolridge said. "He likes to make a lot of noise in the press and try to provoke a reaction from people he's trying to manipulate."

"What kind of reaction?"

"He wants money," Rand said. "His specialty is buying historically or environmentally sensitive property at rock-bottom prices, then threatening to destroy the property or to use it in some offensive way if the government, or sometimes a private conservation group, doesn't step in and pay the high price he demands."

"That's extortion," she said.

"And perfectly legal," the captain said. "If he owns the property, he's free to do almost anything he wants with it."

"That sounds like a story Lauren would want to cover," she said. "Maybe she came here from Denver to interview him."

"Or maybe he contacted her," Carmen Redhorse said. "He likes to use the press to communicate his demands."

"We need to talk to him," Sophie said again,

her agitation rising. They all looked so calm and unconcerned. Couldn't they see how important this was?

"That's not so easy to do," Rand said. "Prentice has a team of lawyers running interference between him and anyone he doesn't want to talk to—in particular, members of this task force. Unless we charge him with a crime, which we have no evidence he's committed, or subpoena him as a witness, the chances of him answering any questions we have for him are slim to none."

More looks passed between them, but these were easier to read. "You may not believe this is worth pursuing, but I do," she said. "My sister did not commit suicide. She wasn't crazy. And if you won't help me find her, I'll find someone who will."

She shoved back from the table and started toward the door. Randall intercepted her. "Don't go," he said. "We'll do what we can to help." He looked at the captain. "Won't we?"

Captain Ellison nodded. "Start by retracing Ms. Starling's steps here in the county," he said. "Do you know where she was staying?"

"I don't," Sophie admitted.

"Canvass the local motels," the captain said. "Rand, you start there."

Sophie had hoped he would assign the woman, Carmen Redhorse, to the case. A woman would be more sensitive, and easier to work with, she thought. Officer Knightbridge, with his frightening dog and gruff manner, was just as likely to scare people away as to persuade them to help. But he wouldn't frighten her. "I want to go with you to talk to them," she said.

"That isn't possible," Rand said. "I can't take a civilian to question potential witnesses."

"Fine. Then I'll start contacting hotels and motels on my own. If I find anything, I'll let you know." It's what she should have done in the first place, as soon as she saw what a low priority the Denver police gave the case.

Once again, Rand stopped her before she reached the door, his tall, muscular frame blocking her path. She tried to duck around him, but he took hold of her arm, his grasp gentle, but firm. "We can charge you with interfering with a police investigation," he said.

"There wouldn't be an investigation if I hadn't come to you," she said, shaking him off. "Can you blame me if I have my doubts about how much trouble you'll go to to find Lauren? Whereas I know I won't stop until I learn the truth."

"Take her with you to the hotels and motels," Captain Ellison said. "The locals may open up to her. But, Ms. Montgomery?"

"Yes?" She turned to face him.

"Officer Knightbridge is in charge. Do what he tells you or we'll have you on a plane back to Wisconsin before you can blink twice."

She glanced at Rand, whose face remained impassive. "All right," she said. She'd play along, but she wouldn't let him stop her from doing what she thought was best for her sister. "When do we start?"

"How about now?" He opened the door and motioned for her to go ahead of him. "The sooner we get this over with, the better."

RAND'S ANNOYANCE WITH Sophie Montgomery was tempered by the undeniably distracting sway of her hips as she crossed the parking lot in front of him. No doubt her nose would be even further out of joint if she knew he was ogling her. Well, she didn't have anything to worry about. She was pretty, but far too prickly. And she was wasting his time. Her sister's connection to Richard Prentice was intriguing, but he doubted it would lead anywhere. Anyone could have a business card—maybe Prentice had sent it with one of his press releases touting his next attention-getting stunt. Lauren might even have had it for years. If it was important, why had she left it back in Denver?

"My vehicle is the FJ Cruiser with the grill between the back and the passenger compartment." He pointed out the black-and-white SUV. "You can wait for me there while I get my gear."

She crossed her arms over her chest. "I should follow you in my car."

"No, you shouldn't. We'll waste too much time trying to keep track of each other. I'll bring you back here when we're done."

She pressed her lips together in a disapproving line, but didn't argue. Even that didn't lessen her attractiveness. She wasn't actress-and-model gorgeous, like her famous sister, but she had a deeper beauty that went beyond the surface, enduring and natural, like the beauty of a wild animal.

And what was he doing wasting time musing on the attractiveness of this woman who clearly found little to like in him? He returned to the headquarters building and retrieved Lotte from the back room, where she'd been napping. As always, the Belgian Malinois greeted him enthusiastically, whipping her tail back and forth and grinning at him. At least here was a female who appreciated him. "Are you ready to go, girl?" he asked.

She responded with a sharp, happy bark. He rubbed her ears and clipped on the leash. Not that she needed it, but since Sophie was clearly skittish around dogs, he'd do what he could to keep her calm.

When Sophie saw them approaching, she turned the color of milk and plastered herself against the vehicle. "What are you doing with that dog?" she asked.

"Lotte is coming with us." He walked the dog past her to the rear of the vehicle.

"Oh, no. I can't ride in a car with a dog."

"She'll be in the back. And she is coming with us. That's not negotiable. Lotte is as much a part of my gear as my weapon or my radio."

"I told you, I'm afraid of dogs."

She looked miserable, but he wasn't going to back down on this; he and Lotte were a team. "I promise I won't let her hurt you. And she'll be in the back of the cruiser, with a grate between us. You can pretend she isn't there."

She looked from the dog to him and back, then took a deep breath. "All right."

Good girl. But he only thought it—she might be insulted if he praised her the same way he did Lotte.

With Lotte safely secured in the back of the vehicle, he climbed into the driver's seat and Sophie buckled into the passenger seat. "Is this your first visit to the Black Canyon?" he asked as they passed the first of the park's eighteen overlooks into the canyon.

"Yes. I've been to Denver a couple of times to see Lauren, but we never left the city." She gazed out at a trio of RVs in the overlook parking lot. "I'm not much of an outdoor person."

"I'll admit the area around the canyon can look a little desolate at first, but there's really a lot of beauty here, once you get to know it," he said. *Just like some people.* "Not just the canyon itself, but the wilderness area around it. The wildflowers are just beginning to bloom, and the sunsets are spectacular."

"If you say so." She angled her body toward him. "No offense, officer, but I'm not here to sightsee. I came here to find my sister."

Right. And clearly she had no intention of getting friendly with the officer involved in the investigation into her sister's disappearance. Message received. "What will you do when you find her?"

"As soon as I'm sure she's safe, I'll go back home to Madison."

"What's in Madison?"

"What do you mean, what's in Madison? My life is in Madison."

"I just meant, what do you do there?"

"I'm an assistant to the city manager."

It sounded like a dull job to him, but he wasn't about to say so. "How long have you lived there?" he asked.

"Five years."

"Are you married? Any children?"

"That is none of your business."

Of course not. He was just trying to make conversation. He focused on driving, both hands gripping the steering wheel. The silence stretched between them.

"I'm not married, and I don't have children. I'm not even dating anyone in particular," she said after a long moment.

"You were right," he said. "It's none of my business."

"What about you, Officer Knightbridge? Are you married?"

Was she asking because she was truly interested, or merely to even the score? "The only woman in my life right now is Lotte." It was a line he'd used before; if the woman he said it to smiled, he figured they might hit it off.

Sophie didn't smile. Instead, she glanced back at the dog, who sat in her usual position, facing forward, ears up, expression eager and alert. He understood that Lotte could be a little intimidating, if you didn't know her. After all, part of her job was to intimidate, even subdue, criminals. "She's really a sweetheart," he said. "And she's had years of training. She'd only hurt someone to protect me."

"I'll keep that in mind." But her grim expression didn't ease.

"Why are you afraid of dogs?" he asked. He

knew such people existed, but he didn't understand their fear. He liked all dogs. And Lotte was his best friend, not merely his working partner.

"I was bitten as a child. I had to have plastic surgery." She indicated a faint scar on the side of her face, barely visible alongside her mouth.

He winced. "I can see how that would be traumatic, but I promise, Lotte won't hurt you. Think of her as an overly hairy officer with a tail."

As he'd hoped, the absurd description made her mouth quirk up almost in a smile. "What kind of dog is she?" she asked.

"A Belgian Malinois. A herding dog, like a German shepherd, but smaller. She only weighs sixty pounds."

"She looks huge to me."

"By police-dog standards, she's on the small side, but she's an expert tracker."

"Too bad she can't track down my sister."

"She might be able to, if we knew the right place to look."

She stared out the window at the passing landscape of open rangeland and scrubby trees. "Where do we start?"

"Like the captain said, we'll ask around at the local motels and hotels, see if anyone remembers her."

"Why didn't you do that before?"

A reasonable question from someone to whom

the missing person was one of the most important people on earth. "I don't want to sound callous," he said, "but with no sign of foul play and no one pressing us on the matter, your sister's whereabouts weren't a high priority. We've had murders and drug cases and even suspected terrorism to deal with. We only have so many people and so many hours in the day."

"Then I guess it's a good thing I came down here," she said.

"Don't think no one cares about your sister," he said. "Remember, that reporter has been trying to find out what happened to her. But she hasn't come up with any new information, either."

"How do you know she hasn't come up with any new information? Maybe she didn't bother telling you because she thought you wouldn't pay attention."

"Oh, she knows we'd pay attention. She's engaged to the captain. If she found out anything important, she wouldn't give him any peace until he followed up on it." He glanced at her. "So you see, we're on the same side here. And maybe we'll find out something useful today— provided your sister wasn't staying with a friend, or camping out."

"Lauren definitely isn't the camping type, and

I couldn't find that she knew anyone here in town—except Mr. Prentice."

"We've been watching his place pretty closely and we haven't seen any sign of your sister there."

She tensed, and leaned toward him. "Why are you watching Mr. Prentice? Is it because he's… what was the word the other officer used—an agitator?"

Prentice liked to agitate all right, but Rand didn't care so much about that. Part of wearing a uniform was knowing some people didn't like you on principle. "Mr. Prentice's estate is an inholding, completely surrounded by public land. It makes sense for us to keep an eye on his place." He hoped that was enough to satisfy Sophie's curiosity. He couldn't tell her they suspected the billionaire was using his wealth for more than investing in real estate and businesses. Their investigations had linked him, albeit tenuously, to everything from drug runners to foreign terrorists. Sooner or later, the Rangers were going to find the evidence they needed to make him pay for his crimes.

"How many motels and hotels are there in the area?" Sophie's question pulled Rand's attention back to her, and today's search for her missing sister.

"A bunch," he said. "But we can narrow the

field by focusing on the most likely places for your sister to stay. She strikes me as a classy woman, so we can move the obvious roach motels to the bottom of the list. Where do you think she'd be?"

She considered the question for a moment, brow furrowed and lips pursed. "She'd probably pick the first nice-looking place she came to when she drove into town. She wasn't the type to spend a lot of time driving around, looking."

"That would be either the Country Inn or the Mountain View."

"No chains?" she asked.

"Would your sister prefer a chain? There's a Holiday Inn and a Ramada closer to the center of town."

"No, she wouldn't care about that, as long as the place looked clean."

He drove to the Country Inn first. Red geraniums bloomed in window boxes against rows of white-framed windows trimmed in white shutters. A water wheel turned in a flower-lined pond near the entrance, splashing water that sparkled in the sun. "Lauren would have liked this," Sophie said.

Rand parked, but left the car running, with the air-conditioning on, to avoid overheating the dog. "Lotte, wait here," he said. "We'll be back in a minute."

"You talk to her as if she understands you," Sophie said as they crossed the parking lot.

"Of course she understands me. Do you have a picture of your sister with you?"

"Yes." She took her phone from her purse and flipped to a shot of Lauren Starling seated in a restaurant booth, smiling at the camera and holding up a colorful cocktail. "I took this when she visited Wisconsin for my birthday last year."

He didn't miss the sadness in her voice. "It's a great picture," he said. "We'll need it to show to the clerk."

The lobby of the motel was busy, with a couple flipping through brochures at one end of the counter, a pair of tweens choosing sodas from a machine and a businessman checking in. The clerk behind the counter was probably a college student from the local university, Rand decided. She had long blond hair, dyed bright pink at the ends, and half a dozen earrings in each ear. When she was done with the businessmen, she smiled at them. "May I help you?"

He showed his badge and the clerk's eyes widened. "We're looking for a missing woman," he said. "Lauren Starling. She may have stayed here about a month ago." He nodded to Sophie and she held out the phone to show Lauren's picture.

"I'm her sister," Sophie said. "This is Lauren."

The clerk's eyes widened. "You say she's missing?"

"Yes. Do you remember her, or could you check your records?"

"I don't have to check the records. She was here. I remember."

SOPHIE FUMBLED WITH the phone, almost dropping it. "Lauren was here? Are you sure?" Her voice shook. Rand put his hand on her shoulder, steadying her.

The clerk nodded. "I recognized her from the TV, but she was obviously trying to hide her identity. I mean, she registered as Jane Smith or something like that, and paid cash for the room."

"You didn't think that was suspicious?" Rand asked.

"Well, yeah, but people do weird things all the time, and you learn not to ask questions." She tucked a strand of cotton-candy-colored hair behind one ear. "Then she met up with a guy, and I figured they were having an affair." She shrugged. "It happens."

"A guy?" Sophie leaned across the counter. "Who was the guy? What did he look like?"

Rand squeezed her shoulder to quiet her. She was going to scare off the clerk, who looked alarmed. He double-checked the girl's name badge. "I promise you won't get into any trouble, Marlee. Just tell us what you remember."

She shrugged again. "He was just a real ordinary-looking guy—early forties, maybe. Light brown hair cut short, not too tall, not too big."

"Did he register also?"

She shook her head. "And that's really the only reason I remember him. I was getting off my shift and I saw him standing with Jane Smith outside her room. Then he took a suitcase—one of those little overnight bags—from his car and went inside with her. That's against the rules—to have someone staying in the room who isn't registered, but it was no skin off my nose, you know? I was in a hurry to get home and I wasn't going to take the trouble to go back inside and report her. Like I said, it happens."

"Why didn't you say anything to the police?" Sophie asked. "Didn't you see the story about Lauren being missing?"

"I knew she wasn't doing the news lately, but they said something about her being on vacation, and then I just kind of forgot. I don't watch a lot of TV and I mean, I wasn't a hundred percent certain it was her, and I didn't want to look stupid—and you're the first people to come around asking questions."

Rand didn't have to look at Sophie to know she was glaring at him. Maybe she was right.

Maybe they should have taken her sister's disappearance more seriously and made it a point to ask questions before now, but there was nothing he could do to change the past. All he could do was try to do a better job going forward.

"Had you ever seen the man before?" he asked. "Or have you seen him since?"

Marlee shook her head so hard her earrings jangled. "I don't think so. But like I said, he was nothing special."

"Was it this guy?" He pulled up a website on his phone that featured an article about Richard Prentice and turned the phone so that she could see it.

She squinted at the photo of a man in his late forties, with thick dark hair, graying at the temples. "The guy I saw was younger, with lighter hair. That's not him."

"Thanks." He pocketed the phone once more. "You've been a big help. We might have more questions for you later. In the meantime, could you tell us when Ms. Starling checked out?"

She went to the computer and began typing. "The reservation was prepaid and she did express checkout," she said. "The next morning. So she was only here for the one night."

"Express checkout meaning she left the key in the room and you never saw her?" Rand asked.

"That's right. I wasn't on duty the next morning, but the record shows express checkout."

"We'll want to talk to whoever was on duty that morning."

"That would be Candy. She comes on at three today if you want to come back."

"Someone will stop by. Thanks."

He could tell Sophie wanted to say more, but he ushered her back to the car. "Maybe they have surveillance pictures," she said. "We could ask to see them."

"We could—and we will. But chances are they're on a tape loop that gets wiped every twenty-four to seventy-two hours. Otherwise the databank fills up with hours and hours of images of empty parking lots." He started the car. "Does the man she described sound like anyone you know? A boyfriend of your sister's? Her ex-husband?"

"Her ex was a big blond, and she wasn't dating anyone. She would have told me if she was."

"Maybe not if he was married, or she had some other reason to keep the relationship secret."

"She would have told me."

She sounded so certain. But how could she know another person so well? Then again, he was an only child. Maybe some siblings were closer. "Everybody has secrets," he said.

"Lauren and I don't have secrets from each other. We're the only family we have left, and we've stayed close."

The fervor in her voice struck a faint, almost forgotten longing within him. Growing up as an only child to older parents, he'd often wished for a brother or sister—someone who would share his background and upbringing, and always be there. "I hope if anything ever happens to me, I have someone like you fighting for me." He meant the words. As much as he still thought they were wasting time searching for her sister, who was probably off in Cancún with her boyfriend, he admired Sophie's determination to find and help Lauren.

The soft strains of classical music rose from the floorboard near her feet. "That's my phone," she said, reaching for her purse. She fished out a pink iPhone and glanced at the screen. "I need to get this."

"Go right ahead." He focused on driving the cruiser through heavy traffic near a school zone, but he couldn't help overhearing her side of the conversation.

"Hello?… Yes, this is she… Oh! Thank you for returning my call… Yes… Yes… Well, as I tried to explain in my message… All right… Yes… That would be fine… Yes… Goodbye."

She ended the call and rested the phone in

her lap, her expression troubled. "Everything okay?" he asked.

"I think so." She turned to him, her determined expression once more in place. "That was Richard Prentice. He wants to meet with me to talk about Lauren."

Chapter Three

Sophie clutched the dash to steady herself as Rand swerved the cruiser to the side of the road, tires squealing and gravel popping as they skidded to a stop. He shifted into Park and turned to face her. From the back, the dog let out a bark of protest. "Sorry, girl," he called. He gripped the steering wheel tightly, radiating strength and more than a little anger. "You told us you didn't know Richard Prentice," he said, his voice low, almost a growl. "That you'd never heard of him."

"I don't!" she protested. "I hadn't."

"Then how does he have your cell number?"

"After I found his business card in Lauren's apartment, I called the number and left a message. When he didn't call back after a couple of days, I figured he wasn't interested." She was not going to let him make her feel guilty about something anyone in her position would have done.

"And you conveniently neglected to tell us any of this," he said.

"Because I didn't think it mattered." She retrieved her purse from the floor and stuffed the phone back into it. "Why are you upset, anyway?" she asked. "Now you don't have to trouble yourself to talk to the guy—I'll do it."

"He wants to meet you somewhere?"

"He invited me to his house."

His glower was enough to make her flinch. All right, she'd had second thoughts about meeting a man she didn't know at his home, but she wasn't going to admit that to Rand, who seemed to think he could order her around.

"I'll go with you," he said.

"Excuse me, but you weren't invited."

"It's not a good idea for you to go to his house by yourself."

She sat up straighter, as if physically stiffening her spine would somehow increase her courage. "Why not? He's rich, not a criminal—or are you the one who's not telling me the whole story now?"

He rubbed his hands back and forth along the steering wheel. They were big, powerful hands, the nails cut short, the skin bronzed. They looked like hands that would be equally at home punching a guy or caressing a woman.

Okay, where had that thought come from? Obviously, all the testosterone this guy gave off was affecting her, and not in a good way.

"We have no proof Prentice is involved in any crimes, but he's a very powerful man and we suspect all his money doesn't come from legitimate sources." Rand glanced at her. "And he's a jerk."

That was all he could come up with? "Being a jerk doesn't make him dangerous."

"It doesn't make him safe, either."

"You're going to have to tell me more than that to persuade me he poses any threat."

The muscles along his jaw tightened, and she could hear his teeth grinding. After a few seconds, he released his death grip on the steering wheel. "This goes no further than this vehicle, all right?" he said.

She nodded. "All right."

"Last month, right after your sister disappeared, we broke up an illegal marijuana-growing operation and human-trafficking ring. The guy in charge had once worked for Prentice, though he swore they had no connection now. We think Prentice was overseeing the operation, but we couldn't prove it. Then, shortly after that, a pilot was murdered after he flew a weapon that had been stolen from the US military onto public land near Prentice's place."

"A weapon?"

"I can't elaborate, but Prentice had links to that, too. Again, we didn't have any proof to tie him directly, but if we're right and he's be-hind these crimes, we're talking about some-body who's proven he won't let anything—or anyone—stop him from getting his way."

"Now you're just trying to frighten me." The tactic was working, too, though she'd never admit it to him.

"You're right. I am trying to frighten you out of meeting with this guy I don't trust as far as I could throw him."

"If I make sure he's aware that other peo-ple—the task force—knows I'm meeting him, he won't try anything," she said. "Right?"

Instead of confirming her evaluation of the situation, he leaned forward and switched on his emergency flashers. "Did he say he knew something about your sister's disappearance?" he asked.

"No. He just said he'd be happy to talk with me about Lauren. He acted like he knew her. I mean, he called her Lauren and said she was a lovely person." The way he'd said it—"such a lovely person"—had been a little creepy, but that was probably just Rand's dislike of the guy rubbing off on her.

"When are you supposed to meet with him?"

"Why do you need to know that? So you can crash the meeting and scare him off?" It would be just like him to charge in, his dog barking and lunging, ruining everything.

"I won't scare him off. And I won't crash the meeting. I'll come as your escort."

"You told me yourself he doesn't like law officers. If you come along, he'll clam up and won't tell me anything."

"We won't tell him I'm a cop."

"Then how do I explain this random guy who invited himself along?"

"Tell him I'm your boyfriend and I'm very jealous and overprotective."

The words sent warmth flooding through her. Hormones again. It was getting pretty warm in this car. Maybe she should roll down the window. "That doesn't say much about me, that I'd hang out with a jealous and overprotective guy," she said.

"Just tell him I'm a friend." His expression softened. "Please. I've got good instincts and I don't have a good feeling about this."

The "please" did it—that and the fact that she was beginning to have her own reservations about a private meeting with Richard Prentice. He was probably harmless, and he might not know anything about her sister, but she should cover all the bases by talking to him, and also staying safe. "All right. You can come with me. But you have to not act like a cop."

"What do you mean by that?"

"I mean, no strong-arming the guy, or firing questions at him. Let me do the talking. And the dog has to stay behind."

He glanced at Lotte, clearly torn. "Nothing says cop like a police dog," she said.

"All right," he said. "But if he makes a wrong move, I won't keep quiet about it."

She sighed. And she'd thought questioning Richard Prentice would be the hard part—he'd probably be a piece of cake compared to handling Rand Knightbridge.

THE NEXT MORNING, Rand waited for Sophie in front of the duplex he rented in the south end of Montrose. Marco Cruz lived in the other half of the building, but he wasn't home today to give Rand a hard time about being reduced to wearing civilian clothes and leaving his weapons and his dog behind, like an ordinary civilian. But, given Prentice's animosity toward the Rangers, Rand's only choice was to make this visit incognito.

Sophie had insisted on driving, too, though it had been Rand's idea to have her pick him up at the duplex—just in case Prentice had someone watching Ranger headquarters. He wouldn't put it past the man.

Her rented sedan turned the corner and glided

into his drive. He jerked open the door and climbed in even before she came to a full stop. "Hello, Rand." She lowered her sunglasses and looked him up and down.

"Do I pass the test?" he asked, buckling his seat belt. He'd dressed in khakis and a blue sports shirt with a subtle pinstripe. Nothing too fancy.

"You clean up nice, Officer." A smile played across lips outlined in cherry red.

"I could say the same about you." In addition to the red lipstick, she wore careful makeup that accented her big brown eyes and beautiful skin. Her hair was up, with tendrils curling around her temples. Her blue dress, of some silky material, clung in all the right places. She smelled good, too, like something expensive and exotic. She looked elegant and beautiful—the kind of woman who would appeal to a billionaire who could have anything, or anyone, he wanted.

He pushed the thought away. Sophie was too classy to go for a lowlife like Prentice. The man might have more money than kings, but money couldn't buy morals. "Have you thought of what you're going to say to him?" he asked as they headed out of town.

"I lay awake all night thinking about it. To start, I want to know how he knows Lauren, and when was the last time he talked to her. I'll ask if he knows why she was in the area."

"It'll be interesting to find out if he really knows anything."

The entrance to Prentice's estate was unmarked by any sign but, unlike other properties in the area, featured a stone guardhouse set back thirty yards from the road and a heavy iron gate. A guard stepped out to meet them. Sophie lowered her window. "I'm Sophie Montgomery," she said. "I have a meeting with Mr. Prentice."

"Yes, Ms. Montgomery, we've been expecting you." He nodded to Rand. "Who's he?"

"This is my friend Jake Peters." It was the name they'd agreed on, in case Prentice had a roster of the task force. Jacob was Rand's middle name and Peters was his mother's maiden name.

"Mr. Peters is not on our list of authorized guests," the guard said.

"I am a single woman and Mr. Prentice is a stranger to me," she said frostily, also as they'd rehearsed. "He can't expect me to come to his house, in this remote location, alone."

"Wait here a moment." The guard retreated to the stone hut and made a phone call. He was back a moment later. "Someone will be along in a moment to escort you to the main house. Wait here."

"How many houses does he have?" Sophie whispered when the guard had walked away.

"I think there are a couple of places where the help live," Rand said.

A Jeep roared down the road in front of them and slid to a stop inches from the rental car's bumper. The driver, also dressed in desert camo, motioned for them to follow, then turned the Jeep and headed back up the road.

They drove up the gravel drive, around a curve and up a hill. At the top, Sophie gasped and stomped on the brake. "You've got to be kidding," she said.

The place was definitely a castle, but more Disney than Dusseldorf. Constructed of gray stone, it featured crenellated battlements, towers and turrets...even a drawbridge, though there was no moat. "It's like something you'd see in Vegas," she said.

"Being rich obviously doesn't guarantee good taste," Rand said. "But I suspect it's another of his ploys to goad the government into buying him out. He tried to get the feds to buy the land and incorporate it into the national park. When that didn't work, he threatened to build a triple-X theater right at the park entrance, but the county passed an ordinance making such places illegal. Finally, he built this monstrosity. I suspect he thought if he created a big enough eyesore, the public would push for its removal."

"But you can't see the building from the road."

"You get a great view of it from the Pioneer Point overlook in the park, though. It actually blocks a view of the Curecanti Needle, one of the most famous natural rock formations in the country."

She shook her head and drove on.

They parked under an arching portico and a stone-faced servant who looked and acted like a bodyguard ushered them into a great hall reminiscent of a medieval stronghold. "Mr. Prentice will see you in the library," the man said, and led the way to a pair of large wooden doors.

The room in question was indeed filled with books, and with a Native-American pottery collection that, if it was authentic, would command hundreds of thousands of dollars. Rand wondered if any of it was legal, or if Prentice had acquired it from the network of grave robbers who ransacked the pueblos.

"This place is a real fortress," he said, standing close to Sophie in the middle of the room. "I saw at least three guards from the hallway."

"You don't know that they're guards."

"Right. Maybe he's recruiting his own football team. Why does one man need that kind of protection?"

"I imagine someone with a lot of money could be a target."

"Or someone with a lot of enemies."

"So sorry to keep you waiting."

They turned as Richard Prentice approached. He looked small in the massive room, with more gray in his hair than in the pictures Rand had seen and a slight paunch showing in spite of his expertly cut suit. He walked forward to meet them, hand outstretched to Sophie. "Ms. Montgomery, I'm delighted to meet you." He ignored Rand completely, which was fine by him. He had no desire to shake this man's hand.

Rand followed Sophie to a love seat upholstered in butter-colored leather and sat beside her. Prentice took the matching chair opposite. "Your message said you're looking for your sister, Lauren Starling. How can I help you?"

"She's been missing since late May," Sophie said. "Park rangers found her car in Black Canyon of the Gunnison Park, but no one has seen any trace of Lauren. I found your business card in her apartment in Denver and I wondered if she'd been to see you."

"I'd heard of her disappearance, but I'm afraid I can't be of any help to you. I haven't seen Lauren in four or five months, at least."

"How do you know her?" Rand asked.

Sophie shot him a pained look. All right, he'd

promised to keep his mouth shut, but honestly, Prentice was so oily and smooth, Rand wanted to put him on edge.

"How did you and Lauren know each other?" Sophie asked, her voice soft, less demanding than Rand's.

"We met at a fund-raiser in Denver earlier this year, to raise money for an orphanage in Guatemala that is a special interest of mine."

Prentice was interested in Guatemala, all right—as a source for the illegal workers he used in his drug and prostitution operations. Some of the victims of the human-trafficking ring the task force had broken up last month had been from Guatemala.

"We ran into each other in the bar after the dinner," Prentice continued. "She'd clearly had a little too much to drink and I was concerned, so I offered to take her for coffee. We ended up talking for quite a while. She confided her troubles to me—the end of her marriage, her recent diagnosis of mental illness and her worries over her job."

He definitely knew a lot about Lauren, though he could have gleaned all that from newspaper accounts of her disappearance. "Did you stay in touch?" Sophie asked. "Have you talked to her since that night?"

"A few times. Just casual phone calls." He

leaned forward, one hand on Sophie's knee. "I hope it doesn't distress you to know this, but your sister was a very troubled woman. She tried to keep a positive face on things around the people she loved, but she was able to let her guard down more with me. I urged her to seek professional help, but she resisted the idea."

Sophie shifted slightly and gave Rand a warning look, perhaps sensing that he'd been ready to take Prentice's hand off at the wrist. "Lauren did struggle with depression, especially in the months immediately following her separation and divorce," she said, the words carefully measured. "But recently she was on medication to control her mood swings and was doing very well."

"Perhaps she wanted you to think that."

"When was the last time you spoke with her?" she asked.

His eyes narrowed and he might have frowned, but his forehead remained perfectly smooth—the result of BOTOX, or merely remarkable self-control? "We spoke briefly on the telephone perhaps a month ago. She called to ask if I knew of any job openings in television. She was convinced she was about to lose her position. She sounded desperate. I wanted to help her, and told her I would ask around. She promised to call me back, but I never heard from her again."

Rand had to bite the inside of his cheek to keep from commenting on the fact that Prentice had failed to tell the Rangers any of this. In fact, he'd denied knowing Lauren Starling at all.

Sophie knotted her hands in her lap. "The last time I talked to her, she said she was working on a new story—something big that would show the station how valuable she was to them. She sounded very excited."

"She never mentioned anything like that to me. What was this story about?"

"She didn't say. I was hoping you'd know."

"I'm afraid I can't help you. I'm sorry." He stood, signaling the meeting was at an end. "I don't mean to rush you, but I have other business I must attend to."

"Of course." Sophie rose also. "I won't keep you. But do you have a powder room I can use? I just need to, um, freshen up."

This was part of their plan, too—to get her into another part of the house to look around while Rand kept an eye on Prentice.

"Certainly. Back into the hallway, and it's the first door on your left."

She crossed the room quickly, leaving them alone. Prentice turned to Rand, his expression hard. "I hope I've satisfied you that I have no designs on Ms. Montgomery's person."

Did this guy rehearse his stilted dialogue in

the mirror? Or did everything he knew about acting come from old black-and-white movies? "Sophie is worried about her sister," Rand said, doing quite the acting job of his own, playing the role of mild-mannered innocent boyfriend. "And your wealth and power intimidate her." Maybe flattery would make him lower his guard a little. "You can understand her wanting a little moral support."

"Since you're such good friends with her, perhaps you can persuade her to give up this fruitless search and accept that her sister has most likely succumbed to depression and taken her own life," Prentice said. "That's what the authorities believe, isn't it?"

"That's what they've told her." What he had told her, though her staunch refusal to accept such a verdict—and Prentice's insistence that she do so—was adding to his doubts. "But she says she won't stop until she's tracked down her sister. That's why she's here, tracing Lauren's last known whereabouts."

Something flashed in Prentice's eyes—alarm? But too quickly the expression was gone. "Lauren did not come to the Black Canyon to see me," he said.

"I'm sorry I kept you waiting." Sophie rejoined them. Her voice was bright, but she was paler than before, and when Rand took her arm to escort her out of the house, he felt her trembling.

Outside, she handed him the keys and walked around to the rental car's passenger side. She waited until they were in the car, driving away, before she spoke. "He's lying," she said. "Lauren has been in that house, and recently. Today even."

"Why do you say that?"

"I smelled her perfume. It's a very distinct scent—Mitsouko. Not very many women wear it."

"Maybe he has a girlfriend who does."

"It would be a big coincidence."

"Coincidences happen." Though less than some people liked to believe.

"Lauren was there. I can feel it." Her voice broke and she turned to him, her face a mask of anguish. "We've got to find her and we've got to help her, before it's too late."

Chapter Four

"Tell me everything, exactly as it happened."

Graham spoke softly, his expression neutral and nonthreatening, but Rand thought Sophie looked ready to bolt. They were back at Ranger headquarters, in the conference room with Graham, Carmen and Simon. The rest of the team—border patrol agent Michael Dance and Montrose County sheriff's deputy Lance Carpenter—had joined them. In her blue dress, Sophie looked like a bright bird in a sea of brown uniforms, but he couldn't tell if her obvious agitation was from fear or excitement.

"I already told you," she said. "Prentice said a lot of nonsense about how upset Lauren had been. Then I excused myself to go to the bathroom and I smelled her perfume. She's been in that house recently. Maybe she was even there while I was there." Her lower lip trembled and she fought to control her emotions. "We're wasting time sitting here. We need to go get her."

"Richard Prentice said he'd talked to Lauren on the phone a month ago?" Graham asked.

"He said 'about a month ago,'" Rand confirmed.

"That's the first time he's admitted even knowing her," Michael said.

"He said they met at a charity function for Guatemalan orphans," Sophie said. "He gave me the impression they were good friends."

"Yet she'd never mentioned him to you?" Simon asked. "Who's going to resist dropping the name of a famous billionaire if he's their buddy?"

"Lauren wasn't like that," Sophie said. "She wasn't a snob. She didn't care how much money you had or how powerful you were. She was as likely to have morning coffee with a panhandler she met on the street as with the bank president."

"But are you sure you'd never heard her say anything about Richard Prentice before?" Graham asked.

"I'd never heard of him before I found his business card in her apartment." She gripped the sides of the chair, knuckles white, as if ready to leap up. "What does it matter if she knew him or how? Lauren was in his house. I'm sure of it."

"He said she was very depressed about her divorce, and afraid of losing her job," Rand said.

"Of course he said that," Sophie said. "He

wants us to believe she committed suicide." Her voice broke on the last word, and she ducked her head. Rand offered her his handkerchief, wishing he had something more to give her—some proof that her sister was all right. She shook her head, refusing the handkerchief.

"I don't think he was telling the truth, either," Rand said, turning to the others. "He was too glib, as if he'd rehearsed what he would say. And he was volunteering too much. Usually, Prentice plays it closer to the vest."

"When we talk to him, he knows he's talking to a police officer," Carmen said. "He thought you were the jealous boyfriend or whatever."

"Are you sure about the perfume?" Simon asked. "Couldn't it have been air freshener or something?"

"Lauren has worn Mitsouko for years," Sophie said. "It's a very distinctive scent, not like air freshener."

Carmen leaned toward her, her voice gentle. "Sometimes, when we want something very badly, the senses play tricks on us," she said.

Sophie stiffened. "Are you suggesting I hallucinated it?" she asked. "I didn't."

Everyone turned to Rand. He gave Sophie an apologetic look. "I don't have a very good sense of smell," he said. "I leave that to Lotte."

"Then your dog would have recognized this," Sophie said. "Anyone would have."

"Where were you when you smelled the perfume?" Graham asked.

"I was in the guest bathroom, downstairs, just down the hall from the library where Richard Prentice met us."

He nodded. "Did you say anything to Prentice about this?"

"No. I'm not stupid."

"I'm not questioning your intelligence, Ms. Montgomery," Graham said. "I only want to be sure of every detail."

"Why are we wasting all this time?" She shoved back from the table and stood. "All this talking isn't going to help Lauren." She fled from the room, heels striking the tile floor in a rapid cadence, the door slamming behind her.

Carmen started to go after her, but Graham held her back. "Let Rand talk to her," he said. "She's spent more time with him. Meanwhile, we need to discuss what we're going to do with the information she's given us."

Rand hurried after Sophie, hoping to catch her before she drove away. But apparently she hadn't intended to leave. He found her in the gazebo between the Rangers' trailer and park headquarters. She stood with her back against one of the posts that supported the structure, staring out across the canyon. He climbed the steps into the shelter and stood a few feet away, saying nothing, letting the silence seep into him, soothing as the warm sun. No RVs rumbled by on the road out front, no tourists talked excitedly as they gathered around the Ranger station. He and Sophie might have been the only people around.

"I still can't picture my sister here," she said after a moment. "It's so empty and desolate."

"Some people find the solitude peaceful," he said. When he was in the city he felt too crowded, unable to hear his own thoughts for the clamor.

"I think it's intimidating." She turned toward him, arms hugged across her chest. "It's so vast, it reminds me of how insignificant we are. How alone."

"You're not alone." He took a step toward her. "We want to help you. I want to help you."

She nodded. "I know I need your help. And that means working on your timetable, not mine. But it's hard. I've been looking after Lauren by myself for so long—I can't flip a switch and stop feeling responsible."

She spoke about her sister as if she was still a child. "When you say looking after her—do you mean because of her illness?"

"Yes. I know people look at her and see a

grown woman with a successful career and everything going for her—but that was just on the surface. Underneath that shell, Lauren was always fragile. She'd be fine for months, even years, and then something would happen to unbalance her. She needed me there to help her through—to be her advocate when she wasn't able to care for herself, to get her the help she needed and just…just to believe in her, when other people didn't. A mental illness isn't like any other chronic condition. If you have diabetes or cancer, people are understanding. They want to help. When it's your mind that has something wrong, most people judge you harshly—as if you'd get better if you'd only try harder."

"In law enforcement, we only see the bad outcomes of mental illness," Rand said. "We get a lot of training that's supposed to help us understand, but I don't know if that's really possible if you haven't experienced it yourself."

"It's been better since she found this new doctor and has been getting the help she needs, but for so long, I've had to be strong enough for both of us."

"Maybe it's time you let someone else be strong." He moved closer, almost—but not quite—touching her. He wanted to put his arms around her and pull her close, to tell her he would protect her, but he wasn't sure how she'd react to that. Maybe she didn't feel the attraction between them that he did. Maybe she was too distraught over her sister to feel anything else.

She looked up into his eyes, and the force of her gaze hit him like a knockout punch. "I believe you want to help," she said. "And I appreciate it. I do. But I'm not used to relying on anyone else."

"You can rely on me." He did put his arms around her then, and she didn't resist, some of the tension easing from her body as he held her. He let his gaze shift to her lips—soft and pink and slightly parted. Lips he wanted very much to kiss…

A flash of red out of the corner of his eye startled him. Sophie took a step back, out of his arms, as a red convertible turned into the parking lot, a woman in dark aviators behind the wheel. Rand regained his composure and nodded toward the new arrival. "That's Emma Wade," he said. "Let's go talk to her."

The captain's fiancée was a tall, curvy redhead who favored formfitting dresses and four-inch heels. She waved to them, then entered Ranger headquarters. Sophie and Rand followed. Inside the trailer, everyone had gathered around Emma, who stood very close to Graham. The captain's normally stern demeanor softened considerably whenever he was around his fiancée, his expression closer to besotted schoolboy than grim commander.

"You must be Sophie." Emma greeted them, both hands extended. "I'm Emma Wade. I've been looking forward to meeting you."

"I'm sorry I didn't return your phone call when you contacted me last month," Sophie said. "I was so upset over Lauren's disappearance, and then I lost your number."

"It's all right. Why don't we sit down and talk?" Emma led the way back into the conference room. The others followed.

"Emma wrote a profile of Richard Prentice for the *Denver Post*," Graham said. "She spent a couple of weeks at his house and followed him at his various businesses. She knows as much about him as anyone."

"Which isn't that much." She made a face. "Prentice is very skilled at letting people see only what he wants them to see."

"Did he ever mention Lauren to you?" Sophie asked.

Emma shook her head. "No. I know they attended some of the same social functions, but he never said anything about her to me."

"Ms. Montgomery visited Prentice this morning, at his invitation," Graham said. "While she was there, she thought she smelled her sister's perfume. In the downstairs guest bathroom."

Emma's eyes widened and she leaned toward Sophie. "Did your sister own a set of cosmetic bags in a pink-and-gold paisley pattern—three bags, all matching?"

Sophie looked confused. "I don't know. I don't remember ever seeing anything like that, but…"

"These looked new," Emma said. "They were full of cosmetics and hair accessories—mousse, hair gel, a smoothing iron."

"I don't understand," Sophie said. "Where did you see these? Why do you think they belong to Lauren?"

"I thought they belonged to a Venezuelan fashion model, but now I wonder." At Sophie's confused look, Emma patted her arm. "I'm sorry. Let me back up and explain. The last time I visited Richard Prentice's house, about two weeks ago, I went into the downstairs guest bathroom. As you know, it's quite a room—steam shower, double vanities, the works. Being a reporter, I'm naturally nosy, so I looked in all the cabinets. Nothing that interesting, until I came to a cabinet that was locked. I couldn't imagine why he'd feel the need to have a locked cabinet like that, so I picked the lock. Inside were those cosmetic bags. I thought they might belong to a woman he was seeing at the time—the Venezuelan model—but it still seemed odd to keep them locked away. So I took a photograph."

"They might have been Lauren's." Sophie's expression grew more animated. "Can I see the picture? Maybe I'd recognize something."

Emma sat back and sighed. "Unfortunately, I lost my phone and I don't have the picture anymore."

"She 'lost' the phone because someone kidnapped her and threw her down a mine shaft." Graham rested his hand on his fiancée's shoulder, his expression grim. "We can't prove Richard Prentice had anything to do with the abduction, but since it happened on his property, we suspect he was involved."

"Maybe that's what happened to Lauren," Sophie said. "Maybe he kidnapped her and kept her cosmetics as some kind of sick souvenir."

"We don't know," Graham said. "But we intend to find out."

"Why can't you arrest him now?" Sophie asked. "Aren't the perfume and the cosmetics enough to tie him to Lauren?"

"They're not," Graham said. "We need more solid evidence. Right now we have nothing to place Lauren at his house. The cosmetics might not be hers."

"I'm pretty sure Prentice knows I saw them," Emma said. "So they're probably not even there now."

"And you only have my word that I smelled

the perfume." Sophie sagged in her chair. "What are we going to do now?"

"We'll start with trying to find the man Lauren met at the Country Inn," Graham said. "We'll take a look at the surveillance video from the motel. Maybe we'll get lucky and find something. We'll ask the clerk to review some photographs, see if she recognizes the man. And we'll need your sister's cell phone number, and the name of her provider, if you know it."

"Of course," Sophie said. "How will that help?"

"We can review her call records in the days before she disappeared. Maybe we'll find a pattern, or someone who knows something about her disappearance."

"What can I do to help?" Sophie asked.

"That's the tough part," Rand said. "You'll need to be patient while we work all the angles. Things seldom happen as quickly as we'd like."

"If you think of anything else that might be significant, call us anytime," Graham said.

She nodded. "I'll do that. And thank you."

"Give Rand a number where we can reach you." Graham turned away.

"I'll be in touch," Emma said. "We can have lunch." She squeezed Sophie's arm, then followed Graham into his office.

"Let me walk you to your car." Rand took her arm.

She hesitated, as if she wanted to stay, but the last thing they needed was her hanging around. Not that he wouldn't appreciate her company, but he didn't need the distraction. Finally, he was able to coax her toward the door. "Where are you staying?" he asked when they reached the parking lot.

"The Ramada. You'll let me know as soon as you find anything?"

"Why don't I stop by tonight and give you an update?" he said. "I might not have much to tell you, but at least you won't have to spend the night wondering what's going on."

"I'd like that." The pinched look left her face. "And thank you. Not just for that, but for all your help."

He put a hand on her shoulder. "Just remember what I said before—you're not in this alone."

Her eyes met his, dark pools that mesmerized him. Her gaze stripped away any mask of bravado he might wear in his everyday life, and seemed to see the real him, the man who wasn't always so sure of himself, but who wanted to be better and stronger, at least for her. She tilted her face up to his, her lips full and slightly parted. It would be so easy to dip his head and kiss her, to find out if the desire that sizzled inside him was something she felt, too…

"I…I'd better go." She stepped back and focused on finding her keys in her purse. She ducked her head so that her hair fell forward, preventing him from gauging her mood, but his own face felt hot.

"I'll call before I stop by," he said.

"Great. Thanks." She moved toward her car and unlocked the door.

"What's that on your windshield?" He moved closer to study the white envelope with *Sophie* inscribed on the front in a looping, feminine hand.

Sophie stared at the missive, her face as white as the paper.

"What is it?" he asked. "What's wrong?"

"Nothing." She snatched the envelope from beneath the windshield wiper. Her eyes widened, and she swayed.

Rand steadied her, his hands on her shoulders. "What is it?" he asked. "Do you know who it's from?"

She covered her mouth with her hand and shook her head, eyes glistening. "It's from Lauren," she whispered. "I'd recognize her handwriting anywhere."

Chapter Five

Sophie stared at the envelope, her name scrawled across the front in Lauren's exuberant script. How many times had she seen that handwriting—on birthday cards and phone messages and reminder notes? *Sophie.* Six simple letters representing the first word Lauren had ever spoken, calling out to her now from the page.

Rand's arm around her steadied her, brought her back to the present, to the parking lot in the glaring sun, the wind tugging at her clothes and hair. "Let's go inside and see what it says," he said, and urged her toward the office.

She let him lead her inside, where the captain, Emma and the others looked up. "What's wrong?" Carmen asked.

"Someone left an envelope tucked under the wiper blade on Sophie's windshield." Rand led her to a chair and she sat, still gripping the envelope in both hands.

"Did you see who left it?" Graham asked.

Rand shook his head. "We were out there

several minutes and we didn't see anyone. Whoever it was, they must have dropped it off while we were all inside."

"It's Lauren's handwriting," Sophie said. "I know it is. I need to see what she said." She started to lift the flap on the envelope, but Rand covered her hand with his own, stopping her.

"Let me," he said. "You don't want to destroy evidence...just in case."

Carmen handed him a pair of gloves, which he slipped on. Then he slid a letter opener under the flap and carefully teased it open. "One sheet of paper," he said, and showed the others. He tipped the envelope, and the paper fluttered onto the table.

Sophie stared at it. "Tell me what it says."

Rand used the letter opener to unfold the paper and smooth it flat. Sophie leaned around his arm to see the words written there. "It's Lauren's handwriting," she said again. "I'm positive."

"What does it say?" Emma asked, moving to stand behind them.

Sophie scanned the words:

Dear Sophie,
Sorry I haven't been in touch but I'm fine.
Don't worry. I've met my Mr. Wonderful
and you know how happy that makes me.

I'll write again when I can. In the meantime, go home and don't worry.
Love, Lauren.

Tears blurred the words; she blinked, trying to clear her vision. When she looked up from the page after reading the words again, she found Rand studying her intently, his expression both sympathetic and wary. "Can I read this to the others?" he asked.

She nodded, and he read the brief message out loud. "What do you make of that?" he asked Sophie when he was done.

She frowned. "It's her writing, and part of it sounds like her, but…something isn't right."

"What's that about Mr. Wonderful?" Emma asked. "Did Lauren mention seeing anyone when you talked to her last?"

"That's the part that bothers me most," Sophie said.

"So she wasn't seeing anyone?" Carmen asked.

"Maybe she met someone after the last time you talked," Rand said.

"It's not that," Sophie said. "It's the choice of words—Mr. Wonderful. She and I had this joke—whenever one of us went out with some guy who was full of himself, we called him Mr. Wonderful. As in he thought he was Mr.

Wonderful and women should be falling all over him." They'd had a lot of laughs over that, sisterly love erasing the pain and awkwardness of bad dates they'd each endured.

"So you only used those words sarcastically," Carmen said.

"Exactly. And the next part—'you know how happy that makes me.' It sounds like she's telling me how unhappy she is." Pain squeezed her chest at the thought.

Rand pulled out the chair beside her and sat. "So you think the message is a code?" he asked.

"I guess you could call it that." She studied the letter again, as if she might suddenly see some hidden message that hadn't yet revealed itself.

"And you're sure this is her handwriting, not simply a good forgery?" Graham moved closer to stand over the table.

"How would a forger know about our Mr. Wonderful joke?" Sophie asked.

"She's right," Emma said. "Most people would say something like 'I've met Mr. Right.' Or 'I've met a great guy.'"

"What about her ex?" Rand asked. "He'd know her handwriting, and he'd know about the 'Mr. Wonderful' phrase, though maybe he took it literally and didn't realize it was an inside joke."

"Have you spoken to Phil?" Sophie asked.

"Not yet," Rand said. "We telephoned his

number and left a message, but we haven't heard anything." The ex didn't seem a likely suspect in the disappearance of a wife who'd given him the divorce he wanted and was paying him support.

"Maybe someone forced Lauren to write this note," Carmen said.

"Someone who knew where you'd be this afternoon," Rand said.

"Do you think someone's been following me?" she asked. The thought sent a chill through her, and she hugged her arms across her stomach.

"I haven't noticed anyone," Rand said. "I think I would have."

She nodded. He'd always seemed alert and aware of things going on around them. "If they weren't following me, how did they—whoever they are—know that I was here? Did they just see my car out front and take advantage of the opportunity?"

"Even if they guessed you might come to the park because your sister disappeared here, they're taking a chance, driving around hoping to spot you," Carmen said.

"They didn't necessarily have to physically tail you." Graham looked thoughtful. "Not if they can track you electronically."

"What is he talking about?" Sophie asked Rand.

Rand's mouth tightened into a hard line. "He's

talking about a tracking device on your car." He stood and she rose also and followed him, along with the others, out to the parking lot. He dropped to the ground and rolled over on his back and slid under the bumper. A moment later he emerged, a box about the size of a packet of cigarettes in his hand.

Sophie stared at the box, on which two lights blinked green. "That's a tracking device?"

"It has GPS." He turned the box over, examining it. "Anyone with a computer and the right program can see wherever you go."

Anger surged through her. She wanted to snatch the box out of his hand and stomp on it. "Why would someone do that?" she asked. "And has it been there ever since I got to Colorado?"

"Someone could have put it on while your car was parked at your hotel," Carmen said.

"Or one of Prentice's guards could have put this on your car while we were inside talking to him," Rand said.

"Then that means I was right—Lauren was at his house. He's holding her prisoner and he made her write the note, thinking it would make me go away." She gripped his arm. "You have to rescue her."

"We don't know where she is." He looked pained as he said the words.

Was he being purposely dense? "She's at Richard Prentice's estate. This proves it."

"This isn't proof." The captain moved to stand in front of her, his expression stern, but his voice gentle. "This proves that someone is following you," he said. "But we don't know who that is. We'll try to trace the origin of this device, but the chances of linking it to Richard Prentice are slim to none."

"But the note…"

"Even if you're right and your sister wrote it, we don't know how it got to your car," Graham said. "We'll question anyone who may have driven by and ask if they've seen anything, but it's easy enough for someone to park at the Ranger station and slip over here without anyone noticing."

"She was in the house. I smelled her perfume." She'd been that close to Lauren. Why hadn't she stayed there and demanded to see her?

"If we go back there now I can almost guarantee you won't find any trace of that scent," Rand said. "If Richard Prentice does have your sister, he's been doing a good job of hiding that fact for the last month."

She covered her mouth with her hand, fighting for control. Was Lauren imprisoned in a locked room or dungeon, like women she'd read about in the papers or seen on TV who had been held prisoner for years, invisible to everyone who lived and worked around them?

"There must be something you can do," she said after a moment.

"We'll put extra surveillance on Prentice's estate," Graham said.

"He'll love that," Emma said. "He's already suing the Rangers for harassment."

"Can't you get a warrant to search his property?" Sophie asked.

"On what grounds?" Graham asked. "Not to mention a billionaire like Prentice wields a lot of influence."

"And he has a state senator on his side," Rand said. "The only way to overcome their opposition is to gather convincing evidence and have a solid case. Which we intend to do."

"How will you do that?" she asked.

"We'll start with the hotel clerk," Graham said. "We'll see if she can identify the man who was with your sister. We know it wasn't Richard Prentice, but maybe it was someone who works for him."

"What am I supposed to do?" she asked.

"Follow Lauren's advice and try not to worry," Graham said, though the sympathy in his eyes told her he knew how difficult that would be.

"Let me help you," she said. "There must

be something I can do—paperwork, phone calls…" Anything was better than sitting around worrying.

"When you go back to your hotel this afternoon, try to remember everything you can about your last conversations with her," Rand said. "Even something insignificant might help us understand why she came to Montrose and what she hoped to accomplish here."

It wasn't what she wanted, but she could see it was all she had, for now. She nodded. "All right. And you'll let me know if you find out anything at all?"

He nodded. "I'll stop by this evening." He handed the tracking device to Carmen, then took Sophie's arm and guided her back to the driver's side of the car. "I know this is hard," he said. "But try to stay strong, for Lauren's sake. This is a priority now. We'll do everything we can to find her."

"You believe me, don't you?" She studied his face, searching for confirmation that he was on her side. "You believe that I smelled Lauren's perfume and I recognized her handwriting?"

"I believe you."

"You're not just saying it to be nice?"

"I work with a dog who can recognize the faintest scents—ones the human nose can't detect. Why wouldn't you recognize a perfume your sister wore all the time? Scent is one of the most powerful senses, and even though we don't have the ability of dogs, we associate certain smells with specific people and situations."

"Are you comparing me to a dog?" She managed a smile to show she wasn't insulted.

"Hey, I meant it as a compliment. I think a lot of my dog."

"I'll remember that." Though dogs frightened her, she wished she had someone she could feel as close to right now.

"Hang in there." He squeezed her shoulder. "I'll see you this evening. Maybe we can go to dinner. It will do you good to get out of the hotel for a while."

"All right. See you then." She slid into the driver's seat and fit the key into the ignition. She'd do as he suggested and focus on staying strong, for Lauren's sake. But she'd never imagined how hard that would be. Today had been like losing her sister all over again.

"WHAT IF WE'RE looking in the wrong direction, and Prentice doesn't have anything to do with Lauren Starling's disappearance?" Marco Cruz, his expression unreadable behind his dark sunglasses, asked the question as he and Rand and Lotte headed to the Country Inn that afternoon.

"Anything's possible," Rand said. "Maybe

it's an incredible coincidence that everything appears to point back to him."

"Prentice knew Lauren," Marco said. "Maybe she even came here to see him. But I don't see any motivation for him to kidnap her."

"Maybe she found out something about his operation that he didn't want getting out."

"In that case, I think he'd kill her. Why keep her around for a month?"

"I don't know, but I hope Sophie's right and Lauren really did write that letter. Wherever she is, I hope she's still alive."

"After all she's been through, the woman deserves a break," Marco said.

"Yeah. She dropped everything to come down here and look for her sister—not many people would do that."

"I was talking about Lauren, but yeah, I can see it's been hard on Sophie, too."

Rand hoped Sophie was able to get some rest at her hotel this afternoon, though he doubted it. She clearly felt responsible for her sister, almost the way a mother might feel about a child. "Do you have any brothers and sisters?" he asked.

"I've got six sisters." Marco folded his arms over his chest. "I'm the youngest."

Rand started to make a joke about the baby of the family, but nothing about the muscular, six-

foot, ex–Special Forces DEA agent said "baby."
"Do they all still try to look after you?" he asked.

"They do. When I was still in California they were always up in my business, telling me what to do, what to eat, what to wear, who to date. I told them I had one mother, I didn't need six more, but they don't listen."

"I guess that could get to be a little much. But now that you're so far away, do you miss them?"

"Nope." He glanced at Rand. "But if anybody tried to hurt one of them, I'd do whatever it took to find that person and make him pay."

Pity the man—or woman—who had to face Marco's wrath, Rand thought. He signaled for the turn into the motel parking lot. Marco retrieved the tablet with the mug shots they'd put together while Rand let Lotte out of the back and clipped on her leash. She gave a big shake, like an athlete loosening up before a race, then looked up at him, wagging her tail. "I don't have a job for you right now, girl," he said. "Just thought you'd like to stretch your legs."

Marlee and another young woman, shorter and rounder with long blond hair, looked up from behind the registration desk when they entered. "What a gorgeous dog," the other woman said. "What's her name?"

"Her name is Lotte." Rand checked the clerk's name tag. "Hello, Candy."

"Hey, Officer Knightbridge," Marlee said, but her eyes were fixed on Marco. "Who's your friend?"

"Marco Cruz." Marco showed his credentials and both women leaned forward to study them.

"What can we do for you, Officer Cruz?" Marlee asked, a little breathily. Marco often had that effect on women. Rand might as well be invisible.

"We brought some photos for you to look at." Marco switched on the tablet and handed it to Marlee. "We want to see if you recognize any of them as the man Lauren Starling met when she stayed here." The tablet started through a slide show of men's photos they'd pulled from the files of the local police of everyone who matched the description Marlee had given them.

"You mean Jane Smith?" Candy asked. "I knew that had to be a fake name—what do you call it, when someone makes up a name like that?"

"An alias," Marco said.

"Right." Candy's smile broadened. "I knew Jane Smith had to be an alias, but I had no idea she was somebody famous until Marlee told me. And now she's missing? That's wild!"

"Did you see the man she was with?" Rand asked.

Candy shook her head. "Sorry, I didn't." She

elbowed her friend. "Usually, night shift is more interesting, but not that day."

"There's a lot of guys here," Marlee said, eyes on the tablet. "So far, nobody rings a bell."

Candy leaned over her shoulder to watch the slide show. "Some shady-looking characters," she said. "I prefer a more clean-cut type myself." She sent Marco a flirtatious look.

"Was anyone else on duty during Ms. Starling's stay here?" Rand asked.

The two young women exchanged glances. "There's Jobie, the handyman," Marlee said doubtfully. "He's always around during the day."

"Is he here now?" Rand asked.

"Somewhere, I guess," Marlee said.

"Could you ask him to come up here, please?"

"I'll call him." Candy moved to the phone.

Marlee began flipping through the photos on the tablet again.

"Take your time," Rand said. "Don't focus so much on what they're wearing or their expression. Try to picture them standing with Lauren that afternoon. Do any of them match your memory of the man she met outside her room?"

"Jobie's on his way up," Candy said, joining them again.

After a few moments a man in his fifties dressed in baggy pants and a University of Denver sweatshirt shambled in. He eyed Marco and

Rand warily, but addressed Candy. "You wanted me for something?"

"These gentleman have some questions for you," she said.

"What kind of questions?" He took a step back.

Jobie looked as if he would bolt out the door if either officer took a step toward him. Rand was used to dealing with people who were nervous around cops. He watched the handyman closely out of the corner of his eye, ready for trouble, but kept his tone casual. "Do you remember a woman who was staying here about a month ago, a pretty blonde, registered as Jane Smith?"

"We get a lot of pretty blondes who stay here," Jobie said.

"This one was in 154, on the back side of the building," Candy said. "Very classy."

He shook his head, his eyes half-closed. "Don't remember."

"Maybe a picture will refresh your memory." Marco handed him the photograph of Lauren they'd copied from Sophie's phone.

His eyes opened wider as he studied the picture, but he shook his head as he handed it back. "Don't know."

"Are you sure?" Rand asked. "We think she met a man here. Did you see her with anyone, maybe talking outside her room?"

Jobie looked at Candy. "It's okay," she said. "You're not in any trouble."

"If you saw something, you need to tell us," Rand said. "If we find out later you lied to us, it could cause trouble."

Anger flared in his eyes, and he shoved the picture back at them. "What's it to you, anyway?" he asked.

"This woman might be in trouble," Rand said. "The man she was with might know something that could help us find her."

"Alan don't know nothing," Jobie said. "He stays clear of trouble."

"Alan who?"

Jobie pressed his lips together and gave a single shake of his head.

Candy leaned across the counter toward him. "Do you mean Alan Milbanks?" she asked. "Was he talking to this Jane Smith?"

"Maybe."

"Who's Alan Milbanks?" Rand asked.

"He's just this guy," she said. "He owns the fish place."

"What fish place?" Rand asked.

"Oh, you know—out on the highway, just past the airport? There's a big sign—Fresh Seafood."

"You go there often?" Marco asked.

Candy flushed. "Not often. I just… I have a friend who likes to go there, and sometimes I go with him, that's all." She turned back to Jobie. "Was it Alan?"

"Maybe."

"Alan wasn't the guy I saw." Marlee looked up from her study of the tablet. "Alan is older than the guy I saw, and his hair is darker."

"Jobie, did you see Jane Smith talking to Alan Milbanks here at the motel?" Rand fixed the handyman with a stern gaze.

Jobie shoved his hands in his pockets and nodded. "Yeah. They were standing by his car, parked in front of her room."

"What were they talking about?" Marco asked. "Did you overhear anything?"

"No. I figured they were just making a transaction, you know."

Rand and Marco exchanged a look. "A transaction?"

Jobie squirmed. "Alan does a little dealing on the side sometimes. At least, that's what I hear. I wouldn't know personally."

I just bet you wouldn't, Rand thought. He turned to Candy. "Is that right? Does Alan Milbanks deal drugs?"

She flushed. "I've heard rumors that he sometimes has stuff for sale. Just, from time to time, you know. Nothing big."

"But you say the guy you saw wasn't Alan?" Marco asked Marlee.

She shook her head, then glanced down at the tablet once more. "I think he might have been this guy here." She turned the tablet around and pointed to a color mug shot of a thirtysomething man with light brown hair and schoolboy good looks. "I'm pretty sure this is the one."

Candy leaned over to study the photo. "Cute. I think I'd remember him."

"Did you see him?" Rand asked.

Candy shook her head. "Sorry. No."

"Are you sure this is the guy?" Randall asked Marlee.

She nodded. "I remember the way his nose was crooked, and that little dimple in his chin. His hair was a little shorter than in this picture, and he was smiling, but it's the same guy, I'm sure."

"Thanks for your help." Marco took the tablet and switched it off. "We may have more questions later."

"You did great," Rand said. "Thanks." He tugged at Lotte's leash and they headed for the door.

"Come back anytime," Candy called. "It's usually so boring around here."

When they were in the cruiser again, Lotte in her place behind them, Marco consulted his notes. "Sounds like Lauren was a busy woman during her short stay here. Do you think she was buying drugs from Alan Milbanks?"

"Maybe a little self-medication?" Rand shrugged. "Who knows?" He punched some information into his computer. "I'm trying to see what I can find out about Alan Milbanks."

"Sounds like the guy was selling more than fish."

"Oh, yeah." He nodded. "It says here he was charged with dealing drugs out of his seafood shop, but the case was dismissed for lack of evidence."

"When was this?" Marco asked.

"About five months ago." He scrolled down the screen, but found no previous charges or convictions for Milbanks. "What I'm wondering is, does he have any connection to Richard Prentice? And how would a guy like that know Lauren Starling?"

"We need to go ask him." Marco tapped the tablet on his lap. "What about the guy Marlee picked out? Anybody we know?"

"That guy is Phil Starling. Lauren's ex-husband."

"I thought he was in Denver. What was he doing in Montrose?"

Rand started the cruiser and shifted into gear. "That's what we have to find out."

Chapter Six

The hotel room might as well have been a prison cell, for all that Sophie was able to relax in it. She kept replaying the scene in Richard Prentice's mansion. What would have happened if, instead of leaving peacefully, she'd demanded to see her sister? Or maybe she should have looked for her on her own, searching the house until Prentice forced her to stop. Had she passed up the chance to save her sister?

A knock on the door interrupted her fretting. Had Rand learned something to tell her already? She hurried to answer it, and was surprised to see not the handsome Ranger, but Emma Wade and another woman.

"We figured you'd be going stir-crazy, stuck here alone in this hotel," Emma said. "This is my friend Abby Stewart. We thought maybe we could take you out for coffee."

"Come in." Sophie opened the door wider and ushered them into her room. "I have been going a little crazy, sitting here worrying about what's going to happen."

"I'm so sorry about your sister." Abby, slim with long, dark blond hair, offered a shy smile. "I remember seeing her on television—she always struck me as so warm and friendly."

"She never met an enemy," Sophie said. "Growing up, she was always outgoing and popular. I was the quiet, bookish sister, but I guess that's why we got along so well. We never competed in the same arena. I rooted for her at cheerleader tryouts and she bragged to everyone she knew when I made the honor society." The memory sharpened the pain around her heart that never really left her these days. Yes, Lauren could be annoying at times, and they'd had their share of sisterly squabbles, but Sophie never thought of those days, only of the good times.

"Abby's a brain, too," Emma said. "She's getting her master's in environmental science or something."

"That's what brought me to the Black Canyon of the Gunnison," Abby said. "I met Michael while I was doing research in the park."

At Sophie's blank look, Emma filled in the details. "Abby's engaged to Michael Dance, one of the other Rangers. And I take it you already figured out I'm seeing Captain Ellison."

"Rand mentioned it, yes." And there was no ignoring the large diamond on the third finger of Emma's left hand.

"You two seem to have hit it off," Emma said. "I was beginning to think the only female he was interested in is his dog."

"Oh, Rand's not...I mean, he's just trying to help me find Lauren." Her face felt hot.

"Still, he's definitely easy on the eyes," Emma said. "I understand he plays lacrosse in his spare time. Those guys always have great legs."

"Um, I hadn't noticed." Well, she had noticed Rand was good-looking. After all, she wasn't blind. More blushing. Time to change the subject. "Should we go get that coffee? I really would love to get away from this room for a while."

"Sure," Emma said. "There's a really cute bakery and coffee shop downtown, and there are some interesting boutiques nearby we can check out afterward, if you'd like. I always say, there's nothing like a little retail therapy."

"That would be great." Anything to distract her from her worries, at least for a little while.

The coffee shop was every bit as adorable as predicted, with gingham curtains and chicken-shaped salt-and-pepper shakers on every table. Sophie inhaled the scents of fresh-baked bread and roasting coffee and felt some of the tension leave her body.

They ordered lattes and cinnamon muffins, and took a table by the window. "Thank you again for taking such an interest in Lauren's disappearance," Sophie said to Emma. "I understand you've really stayed on the Rangers' case about it."

Emma stirred sugar into her coffee, all her earlier cheerfulness vanished. "My own sister disappeared when I was a freshman in college," she said. "The police didn't take it seriously at first, because she'd run off once before."

"What happened?" Sophie asked.

"She was murdered. They never did catch the person or persons who killed her." She reached across the table and squeezed Sophie's arm. "I'm hoping for a much better outcome for your sister. After all, that note means she's still alive."

Sophie nodded and sipped her coffee, waiting until she was sure her voice was steady before she spoke. "I don't know what to make of the note," she said. "I mean, did anyone think I'd really fall for that, without seeing Lauren and talking to her, face-to-face?"

"Someone who's used to everyone doing what he wants might believe it," Emma said as she pinched off a piece of muffin and popped it in her mouth.

"Someone like Richard Prentice?" Abby asked.

"You've both lived here awhile, haven't you?" Sophie asked. "What do you know about Prentice? Would he really do something like kidnap my sister? And why?"

"I've only been here a couple of months," Abby said. "All I know about him is that he likes to throw his weight around, he has lots of money and he doesn't like the Rangers one bit."

"I wrote a profile of him for the *Denver Post*," Emma said. "I followed him around for two weeks and he struck me as a pretty typical powerful businessman with a lot of money. He's smart and arrogant and he's made sure a lot of people owe him favors. But I never thought he was a criminal until I was attacked after visiting his ranch one day, thrown down a mine shaft and left to die."

"Richard Prentice did that?" Sophie stared. The captain had mentioned the abduction, but hearing the details from Emma made it sound all the more shocking.

"He wouldn't get his own hands dirty," Emma said. "But I believe he ordered the attack, to keep me from looking further into goings-on at his ranch."

"Then why isn't he in jail?" Sophie wadded a napkin into a ball, frustration overwhelming her once more.

"Because there's no proof linking him to the attack on me or the crimes in the park or anything," Abby said. "And his lawyers do a good job of keeping the Rangers from getting too close."

"They're going to have to come up with something so damning there's no way he can wiggle out from under the charge," Emma said. "If he is responsible for your sister's disappearance, and the Rangers can make the case against him, it would put him away for a very long time, and probably save a lot of other lives."

"There must be some way to find out the truth," Sophie said.

"If it's there, the Rangers will find the evidence they need," Abby said. "And they'll find Lauren. Believe me, they're putting everything they have into stopping this crime wave. Michael stays up nights, going over and over the evidence they've amassed, trying to find the one thing that will break open the case."

"Graham, too," Emma said. "I used to get frustrated at what I thought was law enforcement dragging their feet. But now I see all the things they do behind the scenes that the public never knows about."

"That must be hard, though," Sophie said. "Being with men who work such dangerous jobs. Don't you worry?"

"We worry," Abby said. "But you can't live your life worrying all the time, so after a while you just put it aside and try not to think about it. This is just your life now and you try to enjoy each day and not angst about the future."

"I need to learn how to do that," Sophie said. For so many years, she'd had to be the strong one in her family, the one who took care of everything, the one Lauren relied on. Even now, when they lived hundreds of miles apart, Lauren would call asking for advice, or for Sophie's help with a problem. She'd made it her job to worry about her sister for so long, she had a hard time letting go of that role, especially now, when Lauren was in real danger.

Emma and Abby filled in Sophie's silence with small talk as they finished their coffee. "I want to check out that boutique next door," Emma said when they were done. "I saw a really cute dress in the window when we walked past."

"You don't mind if we do a little shopping, do you, Sophie?" Abby asked.

"No," she said. "If I see something cute, I might buy it. I didn't bring that many clothes with me."

The boutique did indeed have a number of cute outfits on display, and a large sale section. Soon all three women were combing through the racks, exclaiming over this dress or that shirt, and setting aside clothes to try on. Sophie was debating between two dresses from the sale rack when she glanced up and saw a man by the door, his face turned toward her. Dark glasses hid his eyes, and a ball cap covered most of his hair, but something about him was so familiar, and the menacing set of his mouth sent a shiver up her spine. She took a step back and gave a small cry of alarm.

Emma, who was combing through the rack across from Sophie, looked up. "What's wrong?" she asked. "You've gone gray."

Sophie ducked her head and moved around the rack to Emma's side. "There's a man over there, by the door," she said, keeping her voice low. "He was staring at me. I'm sure of it."

Emma looked toward the door. "There's no one there now."

"But I swear..." She turned, in time to see a man exiting the shop. "There he goes." She pointed. "I swear he was staring right at me, and he looked so menacing—angry."

Abby moved to join them, in time to hear the last of the conversation. "Is it someone you know?" she asked.

"I don't know." Sophie hugged her arms across the stomach, fighting a chill. "He was wearing a hat and dark glasses, but he almost looked like my brother-in-law. Lauren's ex-husband. Except that Phil is usually so neatly dressed. This guy needed a shave and a haircut, and his clothes were rumpled and sloppy."

"Maybe he's a transient—or a tourist," Emma said. "He could have been looking at someone behind you."

"Maybe," Sophie conceded. "And maybe I'm just extra jumpy because of everything that's happened."

Abby slipped her arm around Sophie. "We'll stick together for the rest of the afternoon, and keep our eyes open. If the guy you saw is following us, we'll call the Rangers right away."

Sophie nodded. "That's a good idea. And thank you. For everything."

From the boutique they moved on to an art gallery, and then a bookstore. Sophie began to relax. Maybe the man had been staring at someone behind her. After all, Rand had removed the bug from her car, so how would anyone even know where she was right now? And Phil Starling was in Denver, with his new girlfriend. He wasn't likely to show up in Montrose.

She was scanning a row of paperbacks, searching for a title that might take her mind off her worries, when Emma sidled up next to her. "Check out the guy by the cash register," she said. "Is that the one you saw in the dress shop?"

Sophie turned her head just enough to see the

man, who was studying a display of blown-glass figurines. From this angle, he looked even more like Phil, though a Phil who had let himself go, or who had fallen on hard times. What was he doing in Montrose? "That's him," she whispered. "And I'm sure it's my ex-brother-in-law."

Just then the man turned and looked directly at her, anger radiating from him, as if at any moment he might lash out at her.

But instead of frightening her, his animosity only made her bold. She'd done nothing to deserve his contempt. "I'm going to ask him what he thinks he's doing," she said.

"Sophie, no!" Abby tried to hold her back, but Sophie shook off her hand. She hurried over to the man.

"Phil, what are you doing here?" she demanded. "Are you following me?"

"What are *you* doing here?" The coldness of his glare made her shrink back, but the others had joined her and Abby steadied her with a hand on her arm.

Sophie forced herself to look him in the eye, aware of the stares of other shoppers around them. "I saw you staring at me in the dress shop," she said. "And again just now. If you have something to say to me, say it."

"You need to go home and keep your nose out of other people's business," he growled.

"Does this have something to do with Lauren?" Sophie's voice rose, all the anger and anguish of the past weeks pouring out. It was all she could do to keep from grabbing Phil and shaking him. "Do you know where she is?"

The man began backing to the door. "You're crazy." He looked at the other shoppers. "I never saw this woman before in my life. She's crazy."

"I'm calling 911." Abby took out her phone.

The man turned and ran out the door. Sophie followed, but already he'd vanished in the crowds on the sidewalk.

The other shoppers avoided her when she returned to the store, as if they believed her accuser when he'd said she was unhinged.

"Michael is on his way," Abby said.

"I think you ladies need to leave now." The man who'd been working behind the counter came up to them. "I can't have you upsetting the other customers."

"That man was following us," Emma said. "He threatened my friend here."

The bookstore manager frowned. "I didn't see him do anything but shop, and all he said was for you to go home and stay out of his business. That doesn't sound like a threat to me."

Sophie felt sick to her stomach. To other people, their encounter with the man probably didn't seem like a threat on his part. They'd been the aggressors, accusing him.

"Come on." Emma took her friends by the arms. "We'll wait outside for Michael. At least we scared the guy off."

"For now," Sophie said. "But we made him angry, too." What would he do next time? Or would he take his anger out on Lauren? Had she blown yet another chance to save her sister?

"I DON'T KNOW what you're talking about. I never saw this woman." Sweat beaded on Alan Milbanks's high forehead, and his watery blue eyes looked away—at the counter of the fish shop, at the door, anywhere but at the two officers who questioned him. "Anybody who says they saw me with her is lying."

"I think you're the one who's lying." Rand leaned across the counter at the front of the fish store. The air was heavy with the smell of fish, and the cloying scent of Milbanks's cologne. "You met Lauren at her hotel."

"I meet lots of women," he said, suddenly defiant. "I don't remember all their names. One-night stands, you know how it is."

Rand took in the balding, paunchy man before him, with his sagging jowls and sunken eyes. "Lauren Starling was a real beauty queen," he said. "What would she see in a guy like you?"

"Hey! No need to get insulting." He forced a smile. "I have my charms."

"You got in a little trouble a couple of months ago, didn't you?" Rand said. "Arrested for dealing drugs. Seems you were importing more than fish into your little shop here."

"It was bogus," Milbanks said. "They dropped the charges."

"Maybe you had a little help with that—someone powerful who paid for a good attorney. Maybe someone like Richard Prentice."

Milbanks's face went white, then red. "Get out of here," he said. "You can't come in here harassing a guy trying to make an honest living."

"Is it really an honest living?" Marco asked.

"You got no right," Milbanks said. "Your territory is the park and federal land. This shop is in the city limits."

"Lauren Starling's car was found abandoned on parkland," Rand said. "We're investigating her disappearance. You're the last person known to have seen her."

"Did you two have a disagreement about something?" Marco asked. "Maybe you got a little rough with her and it went too far. Did you hurt her?"

"I didn't hurt nobody." Sweat rolled down Milbanks's face. "You need to leave now. I'm going to call my lawyer." He pulled out a cell phone, but his hands shook so badly he could hardly punch in the numbers.

"We'll leave now," Rand said. "But we'll be back—maybe with a warrant for your arrest in connection with the disappearance of Lauren Starling."

Milbanks looked as if he might faint. The two officers left the store, but stood out on the sidewalk, watching their suspect as he completed his phone call.

"Think he's really calling his lawyer?" Marco asked.

"Or Richard Prentice's lawyer." Rand's phone buzzed and he answered it. "Knightbridge."

"Rand, you need to get over to the Montrose Police Station," Carmen said.

"Why? What's going on?"

"It's Sophie Montgomery. She's been arrested."

Chapter Seven

Sophie didn't know which was worse—enduring the humiliation of being hauled to the police station in handcuffs while a crowd of people, including her former brother-in-law, looked on, or facing Rand when he arrived with Michael Dance and Graham Ellison to retrieve them. "I didn't do anything wrong," she protested when Rand was finally allowed in to see her.

"You're not in trouble," he said. "The guy you were harassing disappeared, and we persuaded the shop owner not to press charges, as long as we agreed to keep you away from his store in the future."

"That guy was Phil Starling—Lauren's ex," she said as she followed Rand and one of the Montrose police officers into the booking area. "He's here in Montrose."

"That explains why we haven't been able to reach him in Denver." He waited while the officer returned Sophie's belongings to her, then took her arm and escorted her outside to the parking lot.

"What about Emma and Abby?" Sophie asked, looking around for her friends.

"They left a few minutes ago with Graham and Michael."

"Thanks for coming to pick me up. I know you didn't have to do that." Rand didn't have any obligation to her—not like Michael and Graham had to Abby and Emma.

"I wouldn't leave you in the lurch," he said.

His expression was so warm, so caring, that she had to look away. Being with Rand always unsettled her. She was definitely attracted to him, but now was the worst possible time to start a relationship, with Lauren missing and Sophie in town for, she hoped, only a few days, until her sister was found.

He grinned. "Nothing like an arrest to bring couples together."

"Not funny." Sophie slid into the passenger seat of the Cruiser. "Don't you think it's significant that Phil is here in Montrose, and that he was so hostile toward me?"

"What, exactly, did he do that was so hostile?" Rand started the Cruiser.

"He was following me and glaring at me. And he threatened me."

Rand glanced at her sharply. "What kind of threat?"

"He told me to go home and keep my nose out of business that didn't concern me."

"What was he referring to, do you think?"

"I don't know. That's what I was trying to find out when the local police showed up."

"Next time you think some guy is following you, call me," Rand said.

"By the time you showed up, he would have left. The store owner was out of line calling the police. It wasn't as if we started a brawl or something."

"Still, you could have been hurt. It's dangerous to confront someone like that."

"I wanted to know what he was doing. And I wanted to know if he knew anything about Lauren—if he'd seen her or talked to her. And what he was doing here. The last I'd heard, he lived and worked in Denver."

"What kind of work does he do?" Rand pulled out of the parking lot.

"He's an actor. Quite a good one, I guess. At least, he had regular work with a Denver theater company."

"But Lauren was paying him support?"

"Yes. She made more money than he did, so the court awarded him monthly support payments." She ran her hand up and down the strap of her seat belt. "I told her she should have fought it, but she was so blindsided by Phil's request for the divorce she was too numb to do anything. And he had a shark lawyer who really went after her."

"What about the other woman? What does she do?"

"She's an actor, too. Glenda Pierce. That's how they met—they were in a play together."

"Do you know if she was with him today?"

Sophie shook her head. "I've never met her. But he seemed to be alone."

"We'll try to track him down and question him."

"Maybe he'll know something that will help us find Lauren. But part of me is afraid to hope."

"Hang in there," he said. "We're getting more pieces of the puzzle all the time. All we have to do is put them together the right way to give us the picture we need."

"What have you discovered?" She half turned in her seat to face him.

"We went back to the hotel and talked to both clerks and the maintenance man. They identified one of the men who visited Lauren at the hotel as a guy who runs a local fish shop, Alan Milbanks."

"A fish shop?" She wrinkled her nose. "What was Lauren doing with him?"

"He's suspected of dealing drugs out of the shop, though local police haven't been able to gather enough evidence to convict him."

"Lauren did not take drugs."

"You sure about that? It's not unusual for people with mental illness to self-medicate."

"She wouldn't do that. She had her prescribed medications and she was very good about taking them. She hardly ever even drinks alcohol."

He nodded and tapped his fingers on the steering wheel. "I'm wondering if her meeting with this guy had anything to do with the big story she was working on."

"That's probably it." Excitement made her jittery. "Did you talk to him? What did he say?"

"He says he doesn't know her and the clerk is lying. But he didn't convince me. We're working on getting a warrant to bring him in for questioning."

"Was someone with him when he met Lauren?" she asked. "You said 'men.'"

"That's another interesting thing we learned. The man Marlee saw Lauren with wasn't Alan Milbanks."

"Then who was it?"

"She identified him as Phil Starling."

Her breath caught in her throat. "So you knew he was in town already? When were you going to tell me?"

"I would have told you tonight at dinner, if you hadn't run into him yourself first."

"Have you talked to him? Do you know where he's staying?"

"Negative on both of those, but we've got people working on tracking him down."

She sat back, letting this information sink in as they passed fields of head-high cornstalks and lots lined with combines and corn trailers, awaiting harvest. "Maybe Richard Prentice doesn't have anything to do with Lauren's disappearance at all," she said, thinking out loud. "Maybe Phil is the one behind it. It makes more sense, really. Didn't I read somewhere that most violent crimes are committed by people the victims know?"

"That's generally true," he said. "But Lauren supposedly knew Prentice, too."

"Not as well as she knew Phil. They were married for almost seven years."

"We'll see what he has to say for himself. Meanwhile, did you think of anything else that would help us? Did you remember anything Lauren said to you about this big story?"

She shook her head. "I've racked my brain, but all she said was that she had a big story that was going to prove to the station how valuable she was to them. She wouldn't give me any details."

"We're going to keep working on this. We'll find her."

"Thank you." She faced forward in the seat once more. "And I'm sorry about the things I said earlier, about you not doing your job."

"Believe me, I've heard worse. Now how about that dinner? I know a great Thai place. Or if you like Mexican…"

"Before we do that, I want to see Lauren's car."

"Her car?"

"Yes. You said it's in an impound lot—that's local, right?"

"Yeah, but what's seeing her car going to do?"

"I just want to see it. Humor me."

"All right." He slowed and switched on his blinker, then executed a U-turn. They headed out of town, past the airport. She spotted a sign that said Fresh Fish. "Is that the fish shop you were talking about?" she asked.

"Yes. Promise me you won't go there and talk to the guy on your own."

"I won't," she said. Though maybe she could stop in sometime. Just to see him, not to talk…

"I mean it," Rand said. "It could jeopardize our case if you interfere. And I don't want to have to bail you out of jail again."

"You didn't have to bail me out." But his teasing tone made her smile. "I promise, I won't go near the place—at least not without you."

The impound yard sat off the main highway, rows of cars behind a tall fence and a locked gate. Rand chose a key from the ring he carried and opened the gate, then drove in.

Sophie spotted Lauren's yellow Mustang, a flashy car for a woman who liked to be noticed. It sat at the far end of the lot, a fine film of dust dulling the finish. Rand stopped behind the car and they got out.

"I can check in the office for the key," he said.

"It's all right. It's open." Sophie pulled open the driver's door, then stopped and looked at Rand. "Is it okay if I look inside?"

"Go ahead. The local cops have already been over it."

She slid into the driver's seat and stared out the window, trying to imagine what Lauren had last seen when she sat here. Had she arranged to meet someone at the overlook and left with them? Had she gone willingly, or been dragged away, kicking and screaming?

She put the image out of her mind and focused on searching the interior of the car. The glove box turned up only the car's manual, a mini flashlight, a pair of sunglasses and the receipt for an oil change dated three months ago. The console was just as uninteresting—a check from a fast-food restaurant, a gas receipt and a tube of lip balm.

A glance at the backseat showed it was empty. Sighing, Sophie sat back and closed her eyes. *Help me out here, Lauren,* she sent the silent message. *Where should I be looking?*

The memory came to her of a trip the two sisters had taken together last year, when they'd driven from Sophie's condo in Madison to the Wisconsin Dells for a weekend getaway. They'd decided to splurge on a spa visit and Lauren had retrieved an envelope from beneath the front floor mat. "Emergency cash," she'd said. "I call it my mad money. If I keep it here, I have it if I need it, but I'm not tempted to spend it, the way I would if it was in my purse."

Sophie bent and pulled up the driver's side floor mat. She had to tug hard, since it was held in place by plastic hooks. Her heart raced when she saw the rectangular white envelope in the center of the space where the mat had been.

"Find something?" Rand opened the door and leaned in.

Sophie picked up the envelope. It felt stiff, as if it contained a piece of cardboard. "I remember Lauren used to hide money beneath the floor mat," she said. "But this doesn't feel like cash."

"Open it, but use the tips of your fingernails, and only touch the edges," he said.

She slid a nail beneath the flap of the envelope, then shook out a single photograph. Rand leaned in closer, his cheek practically touching hers. She could feel his warm breath on her neck, and smell his clean, masculine scent.

She forced herself to focus on the grainy, black-and-white photo of two men talking to each other, standing beside a car in what looked like a parking lot. "Isn't that Richard Prentice?" she asked, staring at the man on the left.

"It is," Rand said. "And the other man is the fish shop owner, Alan Milbanks. Did Lauren ever mention that name to you?"

She shook her head. "I never heard of him until you mentioned him to me."

"He may have been the last person to see Lauren before she disappeared."

RAND AND SOPHIE returned to Ranger headquarters with the photograph. Graham and Michael Dance met them there. "This photo proves a link between Lauren and Alan Milbanks," Sophie said. "And a link between Alan and Richard Prentice."

"Let's bring him in for questioning," Graham said. He studied the photo. "Where was this taken, I wonder."

"Looks like a parking lot," Rand said. "The

photo's grainy enough, it could be a still from a security camera."

Graham passed the photo to Rand. "Give it to Simon—see if he can determine where it came from. In the meantime, you and Michael bring Milbanks in. Let's see if he can tell us more about this picture and his relationship with Richard Prentice and Lauren Starling."

"What can I do while you're gone?" Sophie asked. She was doing a good job of keeping it together, presenting a calm outer facade, but he sensed her anxiety climbing.

"We have copies of your sister's cell phone records. Get with Carmen and see how many of the numbers you recognize." He squeezed her shoulder. Maybe when he got back with Milbanks, they could have that dinner they'd been putting off. He was looking forward to sitting down with her and having a conversation that didn't focus on police work and her missing sister.

"All right. I'll do that." She turned to Graham. "I'm sorry about the trouble we caused downtown," she said.

"Never mind that." He waved away her apology. "Emma said the store owner overreacted. But I can see I need to keep you three women away from each other. Emma can get into enough trouble by herself. She doesn't need help."

Rand left Sophie at his desk, scanning through

the call list from Lauren's cell phone carrier. He loaded Lotte into his cruiser while Michael Dance waited in the passenger seat. Behind them, the dog danced around, panting excitedly. "What's up with her?" Michael asked. "Why is she so antsy?"

"She knows something's up. That she's going to work." He started the vehicle and backed out of his parking space.

"How does she know that?"

"I guess she picks up vibes from me." He shrugged. "Dogs are sensitive. They're attuned to their surroundings in a way we can't even imagine."

Once again, he headed out of the park, back toward town and the fish market. Michael fiddled with the radio, but finally switched it off. Reception was lousy here in the mountains. "So, what do you make of this Sophie chick?" he asked.

Rand stiffened. "What do you mean?"

"Do you think she's on the level, all this stuff about being followed and smelling her sister's perfume and all?"

"Yeah, I think she's telling the truth. Don't you?"

"I was just wondering. I hear sometimes mental problems run in families."

He gripped the steering wheel harder, knuckles whitening. "Yeah, so what's your excuse?"

"Hey, don't be so touchy. I'm just trying to look at this from all angles. Isn't that what we're supposed to do?"

"Sophie's only problem is that she's concerned about her sister, who's been missing a month, and the police have made pretty much zero progress on the case. I don't blame her for being a little upset."

"She got to you pretty quick, didn't she?"

He glared at Michael. "I don't know what you're talking about."

"I'm just saying I recognize the signs. It happened to me that way with Abby—one look and I was a goner."

"But you two had known each other before, over in Afghanistan."

"We met once—and not under the best of circumstances. She wasn't even conscious." Michael had been a pararescuer in the air force's rescue squadron and Abby had been a casualty he'd helped airlift out of a combat zone. When her heart stopped en route, he'd revived her—but she'd remembered none of that until they met again five years later, after she stumbled onto a shooting in the park's backcountry while she was conducting research for her master's thesis.

Rand's relationship with Sophie—if he could even call it a relationship—wasn't on that level.

"I feel for Sophie, that's all," he said. "She's had a rough time of it."

"So that's all you feel—sympathy?"

Sympathy. And a strong physical attraction. He admired her courage and her devotion to her sister. He wanted to know more about her and he enjoyed just being with her. What did all that add up to? "Mind your own business," he said.

"Abby likes her, if that makes you feel any better."

"I'd say Abby has good judgment, except she's with you."

"Here's a little unsolicited advice—if you really feel there's something there, don't be afraid to go for it. Let her know how you feel and see what happens."

"When I need your advice I'll ask for it, which is never."

"Right." Smiling, Michael folded his arms across his chest and closed his eyes. "You can thank me at the wedding."

The image of Sophie, in a white gown and veil, jolted him. But not in a bad way. He shook his head, trying to shake off the wave of unsettling emotions. Dogs were much easier to deal with than women. You always knew where you stood with canines; women were much harder to figure out.

Fifteen minutes passed in relative silence, the

excited panting of Lotte over his shoulder and the hum of tires on pavement calming his jangled nerves. He signaled for the turn into the fish market parking lot and Michael opened his eyes and sat up straighter. "What's this Milbanks character like?" he asked.

"Nervous and suspicious," Rand said. "He was sweating buckets and all we were doing was asking a few questions."

"Let's hope he's not trigger-happy."

Theirs was the only vehicle in the parking lot. The store was dark and empty. Michael parked the vehicle around the back of the building, out of sight of the street. He unloaded Lotte and clipped on her leash, then followed Michael around to the front door. "The hours posted on the door say they should be open until six-thirty," Michael said. "It's six thirty-five." He tried the knob and it turned easily in his hand.

One hand on his weapon, Michael slipped inside. Rand followed, a few paces back, alert for any movement within the store. Lotte strained on her leash, ears forward, tail wagging slowly.

Nothing looked out of place. The shelves of seasonings, cookbooks and a few canned goods were orderly. The coolers full of fish hummed away.

"Mr. Milbanks!" Michael called. "Mr. Milbanks, it's the police. We need to talk to you."

No answer. Michael nodded to Rand. "Check out back," he said.

Rand, with Lotte in the lead, hurried outside and around the building. The parking area here was empty, though the back door to the store stood open. Lotte whined, focused on the door. Rand studied her, recognizing her signal for a find, but her hair wasn't standing up; she didn't sense danger. Cautiously, he approached the open door.

He saw the blood first, a pool of dark red leaking into the doorway. A few feet away lay the body of Alan Milbanks.

Chapter Eight

Rand crouched beside Milbanks's inert body, avoiding the pool of blood. Michael joined him from the front of the store. Rand leaned over and felt for a pulse at the man's throat, already knowing he wouldn't find one. "He hasn't been dead long," he said. "He's still warm."

"I checked the cash register," Michael said. "The drawer is full."

"This doesn't look like a robbery." Rand studied what was left of Milbanks's head. "More like an assassination. Close range. Somebody sending a message."

The jangle of bells made them both start. Rand stood, withdrawing his weapon as he rose. He and Michael took up positions on opposite sides of the room and started toward the front of the store.

"Hello?" a man's voice called. "Alan? Anybody home?"

Rand moved to where he could see through the passage into the front. A disheveled man in baggy cords and a sweatshirt, dirty blond hair falling into his eyes, stood in the middle of the shop. Phil Starling.

Rand stepped into the front room, his weapon fixed on Starling. "Police. Keep your hands where I can see them."

Starling turned the color of sour milk and inched his hands into the air. "Wh-what's going on?"

"I'll need to see some ID." Rand approached slowly. Out of the corner of his eye, he saw Michael moving up on the other side of the room.

"In my right back pocket." Starling stared at Rand's weapon, mesmerized.

"Take it out slowly."

Starling did so and extended the open wallet toward Rand. "I just came in to buy some fish," he said.

"How do you know Alan Milbanks?" Rand checked the ID. Phillip Starling, with a Denver address.

"Who?"

"Alan Milbanks. You called for Alan when you entered the store."

His smile was weak and lopsided. "I didn't know his last name. Just Alan. He…he introduced himself when I was in here last week."

"You buy a lot of fish, do you?" Rand returned the wallet to Starling.

"Yeah, I do. It's good for you, you know."

Starling's sickly pallor and unkempt appearance didn't mark him as a healthy living aficionado. "When was the last time you saw Alan?"

"Last time I bought fish. Maybe, I don't know—a couple of days ago. Why are you asking me all these questions? Is something wrong?"

"Your license has a Denver address. What are you doing in Montrose?"

"I'm here on vacation." He shoved the wallet back into his pocket. "You know, see the Black Canyon, do some hiking, like that."

"Where are you staying?"

"Why do you need to know?" Starling's expression turned surly. "Like I told you, I just came in to buy some fish. I didn't do anything wrong."

"We may need to get in touch with you. Where can we reach you?"

Starling pressed his lips together, in the expression of a pouting child, then heaved a sigh and gave the address of a cheap motel on the west side of town.

"You seem nervous, Mr. Starling," Rand said. "Any reason for that?"

"You're joking, right? I come in to buy some fish for dinner and suddenly I'm being grilled by cops. Who wouldn't be nervous?"

"Are you related to Lauren Starling?" Michael asked the question, startling the actor, who seemed to have forgotten he was there.

"She's my ex-wife," he said.

"When was the last time you saw her?"

"In court, the day we finalized the divorce. Almost three months ago."

"You haven't talked to her since then?"

"No."

"When did you arrive in Montrose?"

He hesitated. Because he resented the question, or because he needed time to think up a lie? "A week, maybe ten days ago. I don't remember."

"You don't remember?"

"It's a vacation, you know. It's not about keeping track of time."

"We'd like you to come down to the station and answer a few questions for us," Rand said.

"I've already been answering your questions."

"Yes, but we have a few more for you, and we'd like to talk to you where we can all sit down and get comfortable."

"No. You don't have any reason to hassle me this way. I just came in here to buy fish and you guys are giving me a hard time." He started to turn and walk away, but Michael was on him in a flash, twisting his arm and bringing him to his knees.

Starling howled and swore. "What do you think you're doing?"

"What do you think you're doing with this?" Rand gingerly pulled a pistol from the back waistband of Starling's cords. The snub-nosed revolver dangled from his index finger. He sniffed the barrel and shook his head. The gun didn't smell to him as though it had been fired recently, but he'd leave the final determination to the experts.

"I got a right to carry that," Starling protested.

"So you have a carry permit?" Michael asked.

"No, but I have a right to protect myself."

"Do you think buying fish is a particularly dangerous activity?" Rand asked.

"In some neighborhoods, it could be. I like to be careful."

"So do we, Mr. Starling, which is why we're going to take you in for questioning and booking."

"You can't arrest me." Starling's voice rose. "I haven't done anything wrong. What are you charging me with?"

"We'll start with carrying an illegal concealed weapon." Rand pulled the actor's arms behind his back and snapped on a pair of cuffs. "From there we might move on to kidnapping, or even murder."

"ALAN MILBANKS IS DEAD?" Sophie stared at Rand, who met her at Ranger headquarters the next morning with the news. She'd planned to spend the morning with Carmen, trying to put names to the rest of the list of numbers Lauren had called in the days before her disappearance. Some of the numbers were easy to identify. Lauren had made calls to her office, her hairdresser, her doctor's office and Sophie. One of the numbers had surprised Sophie. In the days before she'd gone missing, Lauren had spoken to her ex-husband, Phil, three times.

But none of the numbers on Lauren's phone records had a Montrose exchange. The news that one of the few people they knew Lauren had spoken to in town was dead shook her. "Did he have a heart attack or something?"

"He was murdered. Shot in the head."

She took a deep breath, trying to remain calm and take it all in. "Was it a robbery?" she asked. "Or something to do with drugs? You said he might be dealing drugs."

"It could be related to drug activity." Rand spoke softly, his eyes locked to hers. "Or it could be because someone saw us questioning him earlier and didn't want him to tell us what he knew."

"Do you think Richard Prentice did this?" she

asked. "Because of the photograph showing him with Mr. Milbanks?"

Rand settled into the chair beside her at the conference table, where they'd retreated to talk privately. "Richard Prentice is hosting a fundraiser for Senator Mattheson in Denver today." He slid over a copy of the *Denver Post* with a photograph of the senator and the billionaire smiling and shaking hands.

"That doesn't mean he couldn't have ordered someone else to do his dirty work," Rand said.

"What will you do now?" Sophie asked.

"We're working with the local police to investigate the crime scene. There are no security cameras and everything had been wiped pretty clean, but maybe we'll find something. Someone driving by might have seen something. But we did arrest someone on the scene for questioning."

"Who is that?"

"Your former brother-in-law, Phil Starling."

Her eyes widened. "You think Phil had something to do with Alan Milbanks's murder?"

"He showed up right after we discovered the body. He said he'd come in to buy fish, but he was acting awfully nervous for an innocent shopper, and he knew Milbanks's name before we mentioned it. And he was carrying a gun."

"A gun?" She shook her head. "This is crazy."

"Do you know if he has a history of drug

use?" Rand asked. "Did Lauren ever mention anything like that?"

"No. I mean, I may have heard him mention smoking a joint a couple of times, but never anything more than that. He liked to have a few drinks—a few too many drinks, sometimes, but drugs?" She shook her head again. "Did you ask him about Lauren?"

"He said he hadn't seen her since the divorce, and that he'd only been in Montrose a week or so. We're following up on that, trying to find out where he's been staying."

"What else did he say?"

"Nothing. As soon as we got him to the station, he demanded to see his lawyer and clammed up. The lawyer will be here later this morning, so we'll talk to him then. He might feel more cooperative after he's spent a night in jail."

Would she feel more comfortable, knowing her former brother-in-law was in jail? "Do you really think Phil had something to do with Lauren's disappearance?" she asked.

"I don't know. He's a hard guy to read. No surprise, I guess, considering he's an actor."

Sophie thought all men were hard to read, even Rand. Was he spending so much time with her because he truly liked her, or merely because she was part of his case? Or maybe the captain had ordered him to keep an eye on her, despite his protestations to the contrary. After all, everyone who had a connection with Lauren was probably a suspect in her disappearance.

All right, enough with the paranoia already, she thought. Instead of wondering about Rand's motives, maybe she should try to get to know him better.

"Why did you want to be a police officer?" she asked.

"I really wanted to be a park ranger," he said. "I like the outdoors, but, at least for national parks, a law enforcement background is helpful. Then I got on with the Bureau of Land Management and it was a good fit—the outdoor lifestyle I wanted, and the chance to make a real difference."

Her own job didn't make a difference to anyone, she thought. "I wanted to be a librarian," she said. "But those jobs are hard to come by. Business seemed a more sensible choice."

"And you're a sensible person."

She looked away.

"Hey." He touched her shoulder lightly. "I didn't mean that as an insult. I think it's a good thing."

"Sure." Again, she didn't know how to read him. "Would you like to, um, get something to eat? I mean, go to lunch?" she asked. They'd never made it to dinner last night, something that had disappointed her more than she liked to admit. Would he think she was coming on to him, or worse—trying to bribe him or something?

"I'd like that. A lot. But can I take a rain check? I have a feeling I'm going to be pulling a long shift today."

"Sure." She stood, almost knocking her chair over in her haste. "I'll just get out of your way and let you get back to work."

"You don't have to rush off." He smiled, that genuine, warm look that made her insides turn to pudding. Or maybe something warmer and sweeter—hot fudge.

"Sophie?"

"Mmm?" She snapped back to attention.

"Are you okay?"

"Sure. I'm great."

"You look a little flushed."

"It's a little warm in here." She fanned herself. "I'll be fine. See you later." The rest of the phone records would have to wait. She turned and ran from the room. *Get a grip,* she scolded herself as she hurried to her car. Lauren would never have lost her cool with a man that way. Even when she'd been devastated by Phil's behavior, she'd never let him see her pain. She knew how to hide her emotions from the people she cared about.

Oh, Lauren, Sophie thought. *I always thought*

you needed me more than anyone else, because I was the only one you could really be yourself with. But now I need you, sister. I'm not as strong as we both thought.

Chapter Nine

In the harsh fluorescent lighting of the interrogation room of the Montrose Police Station, Phil Starling looked even sicklier and more disreputable. "You don't have any right to hold me like this," he said, as soon as Rand and Marco entered the interrogation room. "I didn't do anything wrong."

"You were carrying a concealed weapon without a permit," Rand said. He laid a file on the table and pulled out a chair. "We just have a few questions for you."

Starling turned to the man beside him—a white-haired, florid-faced fiftysomething lawyer in a paisley tie and rumpled suit. "Tell them they can't hold me."

"If my client answers your questions, are you willing to strike a deal for his release?" the lawyer asked.

"That's the district attorney's decision, not mine," Rand said.

"I'm sure the DA will consider your opinion in the matter," the attorney said.

"I see you haven't met our DA."

The lawyer frowned. "If you aren't going to make a deal, why should my client cooperate at all?"

"How about in the interest of justice? Or because it's the right thing to do? Or how about this one—we want to find the person who's responsible for several crimes. If that person isn't your client, maybe he should help us figure out who it is."

"What crimes?" Starling asked.

"We'll get to that." Rand sat in the chair across from Starling and his lawyer. "Why were you at the fish store yesterday afternoon?" he asked.

"I told you—I wanted to buy fish."

"What kind of fish?"

"I don't know. Tuna, I guess."

"You weren't there to buy drugs?"

"You don't have to answer that," the lawyer said.

Phil's gaze slid sideways. "No."

"But you were aware that Alan Milbanks sold drugs?"

He hesitated. "I might have heard some things. But that's not why I was there."

"Did your ex-wife buy drugs from Alan Milbanks?"

This question got a surprised snort from him. "Lauren? Is that what she's into now?"

"Do you think your ex-wife takes drugs?"

"Nothing that woman does would surprise me. You know she's crazy, right? Certifiable. She even spent some time in the loony bin."

"The loony bin?"

"The psych ward. Mental hospital. Whatever the politically correct term is these days."

"Was that why you divorced, because of her mental problems?"

"That, and a lot of other things." Another sideways glance.

"When was the last time you saw Lauren Starling?"

"You don't have to answer that one, either," the lawyer said.

"A lot of help you are," Starling said. "I don't have to answer any of these questions." He turned back to Rand. "I told you. In court, when we officially split."

"You haven't seen her since?"

"No."

"How does she make the court-ordered support payments to you?"

He wiped one hand across his face, which was shiny with sweat, and glanced at the lawyer, who shrugged, arms crossed over his chest. Starling sighed and turned back to Rand. "So you know about that, do you?"

"The court ordered Lauren to pay monthly

support payments to you as part of the divorce settlement. How did she make those payments?"

He settled back in his chair, as if hunkering down for the long haul. "She mailed a check. Though she wasn't always on time, I can tell you that."

"What happened when the checks were late?"

"I'd call and tell her she'd better get the check to me right away or I'd see her in court."

"But you told us earlier you hadn't talked to your ex-wife since the divorce."

He frowned. "Did I? Well, it's not like we were having a friendly conversation or anything, you know. We just talked about the money."

"What about the money, Mr. Starling? How are you doing financially?"

"That's none of your business," he snapped.

Rand paged through the file he'd brought with him. "You're staying at one of the cheapest motels in town. The manager tells me you're late with this week's payment. And he says you've been there two weeks."

"He'll get his money."

"When was the last time you worked as an actor?"

"I was in a show in the spring. *Barefoot in the Park*. I got great reviews. Right now I'm waiting for a deal we've got going with Hollywood to come through. I thought it would be good to take a little vacation while I had some downtime, because I can see things are going to get really busy here soon."

"But right now you don't have any money coming in?" Rand said.

"I have some savings."

"But your only reliable income is the support payments from your ex-wife."

He snorted again. "I wouldn't call those reliable. She hasn't paid me anything in almost two months."

"You are aware, Mr. Starling, that Lauren Starling has been missing for more than a month."

"I know she hasn't sent me a check and she hasn't bothered to show up for work."

"What do you think happened to her?"

He shrugged. "Like I told you. She's nuts. She probably decided to run off to Baja or join a commune or something. No telling."

"But you haven't heard anything from her?"

"I told you, no!"

Rand leaned across the table and fixed Starling with a cold gaze. "We have a witness who says she saw you and Lauren together at a hotel here in Montrose."

Phil flinched, a reaction so brief anyone who wasn't watching him closely might have missed it. "What—you think we were still sleeping together? Fat chance of that."

"I didn't mention sex," Rand said. "This witness says you were talking. What were you talking about?"

He looked away and said nothing.

"The hotel has security cameras," Rand said. "I'm sure we can find photographs to prove you were there, in addition to the eyewitness." He was sure of no such thing, but he wanted Starling to worry.

"I went by there to talk to her about the support payments," he said, the words coming out in a rush.

"What about the payments?" Rand asked.

"I needed more money." He twisted his hands together on the table in front of him. "She had it good—cushy job with that news station in Denver. Prime-time news anchor, everybody's sweetheart. I got work coming—a big, important role. But everything in Hollywood takes time, so it's gonna be a while before the money comes in. So I figured, she could pay me a little more now, and when the money starts rolling in for me, I'll cancel the payments altogether. If that's not generous, I don't know what is."

"Did Lauren tell you her job at the news station was in jeopardy? That she might be laid off soon?"

"As if that was ever going to happen. That was just an excuse. The station wouldn't dare get rid of her. I mean, she has a disability, right? They fire her, she could sue. Of course, that might not be so bad. Maybe she'd get even more money. Either way, she could afford to share some of the wealth with me."

"But she refused to pay you."

"She did. I even threatened to take her back to court, but she didn't care. She told me she couldn't help and showed me the door."

"How did you feel about that? Especially after you came all this way to plead with her."

"How do you think I felt? I was plenty irate. I told her that wouldn't be the last she heard from me on the issue."

"So the two of you argued. Maybe things got out of hand?" Rand leaned closer, his voice low, confiding. "What happened? Did you hit her? Did she fall and hit her head? Maybe you got scared and decided the best thing to do was to hide the body, drive her car out to the park and make it look like she'd committed suicide?"

Starling stared at Rand, his jaw gone slack, eyes wild with terror. "What are you talking about? I didn't hurt her. I didn't lay a finger on her. I left—told her I'd come back the next day, after she'd had more time to think about my offer. Only when I came back, she wasn't there. I figured she was avoiding me. I haven't seen her since."

"Yet you stayed in town. Why is that?"

"Maybe I like it here."

"And maybe you have people in Denver who are after you to pay money you owe them?"

"Yeah, maybe some of that, too. But I've just been hanging out. I haven't seen a hair of Lauren's since that one day I talked to her."

"What about Lauren's sister, Sophie?" Rand asked.

His eyes narrowed. "What about her?"

"She says you threatened her when you saw her in town yesterday."

"That little mouse? You've met her, right? Can you even believe she's Lauren's sister? The two are nothing alike."

"Why did you tell her to go home and mind her own business?"

"Because she was giving me the stink eye." He drew himself up, indignant. "She never did like me, always treated me like I was something the cat dragged in. The police arrested her for harassing me, remember. I didn't do anything."

"What did she say to you?" Rand asked.

"She accused me of following her. As if I'd waste my time on a nothing like her."

Rand had to fight not to defend Sophie from Starling's disparagement. She was worth far more that all the beautiful, sparkling, empty-headed women he'd ever met. But better to change the subject. "So you didn't know that Lauren knew Alan Milbanks?" he said.

"Lauren and Alan?" He laughed. "He wasn't exactly her type, you know?"

"What do you mean?" Rand asked.

"Lauren might be whacko, but she was hot. She never had trouble attracting good-looking guys. That's why she married me, you know?"

Behind them, Marco coughed. Starling scowled at him but was smart enough not to comment. "So Lauren didn't introduce you to Alan Milbanks?"

"No. I wanted some fish and people told me he had the best fish in town."

Substitute *crack* or *meth* for *fish* and Starling might be telling the truth, Rand thought.

"Do you always carry a gun when you shop for fish, Mr. Starling?" he asked.

"I told you I'd heard rumors about the other business they did at that place. I wasn't taking any chances." He rubbed his hand across his chin, the beard stubble making a rasping noise. "So, what happened—did you finally catch him in the act? Is that why the place was closed?"

"Mr. Milbanks is dead," Rand said.

Starling froze. "Dead? What happened? Did he have a heart attack or something?"

"He was murdered. Do you know anything about that?"

Starling gaped, openmouthed. He certainly

appeared shocked by the news, but after all, he was an actor. Rand didn't trust the reactions of someone who was trained to portray emotions. "Do you know anything about the murder of Alan Milbanks?" he asked again.

"No! What kind of guy do you think I am?"

"A guy who carries a gun to buy fish," Rand said drily.

"I never even fired that gun!" Starling protested. "I bought it off a kid in Denver, for self-protection. I'm not a murderer!"

Fortunately for Starling, tests on the weapon backed up this assertion. The little revolver hadn't been fired in a long time, judging by its condition. And the caliber didn't match the bullet that had killed Alan Milbanks. "Do you know anybody who would want Alan Milbanks dead?" Rand asked.

"How the hell should I know? Somebody he sold bad fish to? I hardly knew the guy. He probably had lots of enemies."

"Why do you say that?"

"Who doesn't have enemies, right?"

"Did Lauren have enemies?"

"Lauren?" The hardness around his eyes softened a little. "Nah. Everybody liked Lauren. Even at her wackiest, she was never mean.

Even when she drove you nuts, you couldn't stay mad at her."

"But you could stay mad at her," Rand said. "You were angry enough to come all the way to Montrose to confront her."

"I told you, that was about the money." He leaned forward, hands clasped, expression earnest. "Listen, I know I was no angel in our marriage. I cheated on her, but you got to understand what it was like being married to her. The big TV star. The beauty queen. Everywhere we went, people fawned on her. If she came to one of my performances, everybody paid attention to her, not me."

"A little hard on the ego," Rand said.

"Exactly. It gets to a guy, you know? And then, I never knew what she was going to be like from day to day. One day she was this dynamo, racing around from one project to another, all happy and energetic, little Miss Positive. The next day she wouldn't even talk to me. She was like this little dark cloud huddled in the apartment. I couldn't depend on her. It drove me crazy. And it drove me into another woman's arms." He shrugged. "So sue me. I'm human. But even after all that, part of me still loves her. I just couldn't live with her."

"The last time you saw Lauren, what was she like?"

"She was fine. As normal as she ever got, anyway."

"Did she seem depressed? Upset about anything?"

"No. Believe me, you couldn't miss one of her black moods. When she and I talked at the motel, she was all business, but not negative."

"Did she say why she was in Montrose?"

"She mentioned something about work—some story she was reporting on—but she didn't go into detail. To tell you the truth, I didn't care. All I wanted was to come to some agreement on the money and leave. She's not really a part of my life anymore, and I always believed in making a clean break, you know?"

"And you never spoke to her again? No phone calls or texts or any other communication?"

"Nope. I called the hotel the next day and they told me she'd checked out. I drove by a couple of times to make sure and her car wasn't in the lot. She didn't answer my texts or calls to her cell. I figured she was on assignment somewhere else and was avoiding me."

"Did that upset you?"

"Do I look like an idiot? Of course it upset me. But I just figured there was no reasoning with the woman. It was time to get out the big guns. I called my lawyer and told him to petition the court for an increase in support. She could afford it, and since I didn't have any income at the moment, I figured I'd get it. She had plenty to spare."

"And did you petition the court?" Rand asked the attorney.

The man started, as if out of a stupor. "Excuse me?"

"Not this guy," Starling said. "My divorce attorney. I just picked this guy out of the phone book. It's not like I've been in trouble with the law before. Well, maybe a DWAI once, but that was years ago."

"I'm sorry to interrupt this lovely chat," the lawyer said, glaring at his client. "But unless you're going to charge my client with something more than this minor weapons violation, I suggest you let him go."

"A weapons violation isn't a minor charge," Rand said. "Your client can go back to his cell and wait until the judge either sets or denies bail at his arraignment tomorrow."

Starling opened his mouth to say something, but a quelling look from the lawyer silenced him. Rand pushed back his chair and stood. "Is there anything else you'd like to tell us about your wife or Alan Milbanks, Mr. Starling?" he asked.

"I hope Lauren's okay," he said. "Really, I do.

She has her problems, but she isn't so bad, really. She doesn't deserve any more hard luck in her life. And if you see her, you can tell her I said so."

Rand left the room as a bailiff came to escort Starling back to his cell. Marco followed him out. "What do you think?" Rand asked.

"I don't think he's telling the truth about his relationship to Milbanks," Marco said. "Ten dollars says one of the reasons he's in such financial straits is that he's keeping up a drug habit. I'm guessing one of the reasons he's stayed in Montrose is that Milbanks was a good source."

"Maybe he's hiding out from the dealers he owes in Denver."

"Probably. As for Lauren Starling—I don't know. I can see things getting out of hand with her, especially if she had a history of erratic behavior that pushed his buttons. Things went too far and he killed her. Maybe accidental, but then he covered things up."

"Except that doesn't explain the note on Sophie's car."

"Maybe he learned she was in town and decided this was a chance to elaborate on the fiction that she'd run away. He was married to Lauren, so he knew her handwriting, the things she would say. He's got a big ego, so he's convinced he can pull this off, divert attention from anyone looking for a body."

"Maybe." Marco pulled his keys from his pockets. "Back to headquarters?"

"I'll meet you there later. I think I'm going to nose around the hotels in town a little more to see if I can find out more about what Starling—and Lauren—might have been up to."

A DAY SPENT alternately watching bad TV and flipping through outdated magazines scavenged from the lobby, while waiting for the phone to ring with word about Lauren, left Sophie on edge. She paced the floor and gnawed at a thumbnail, picking up the phone half a dozen times to call Rand and ask if he had any news, then setting it aside. If he knew anything, he'd call her, wouldn't he?

Frustrated with her own impotence, she sat down at the one small table by the window and opened her notebook. Maybe if she made a list of things she could do to help find Lauren, she'd feel better. She uncapped the pen and wrote *1* Then stared for a long moment, her mind blank.

A knock on the door startled her. She checked the peephole, and her heart gave a lurch when she recognized Rand. He wasn't in uniform this evening, instead dressed in tight, dark jeans, boots and a pin-striped Western shirt that reminded her again of an old-west cowboy—only this one had cleaned up to come to town.

She undid the chain on the door and pulled it open. "Hello, Rand," she said.

"I thought I'd see if I could cash in that rain check on dinner."

"Oh, uh, well…" Having dinner with him didn't feel like the safest way to spend the evening, either. Being near him distracted her from her purpose more than she wanted. Still, she couldn't think of a way to refuse without being rude, and the thought of sitting alone in her room until she was exhausted enough to sleep depressed her.

"I should change," she said, looking down at her rumpled jeans and blouse.

"You look fine," he said. "Great."

She wasn't used to such flattery, but maybe he was just trying to reassure her. "Just give me a minute," she said, and retreated to the bathroom.

She returned a few moments later, wearing a fresh blouse, with her hair combed and lips glossed. "Even better," he said, and opened the door.

As she approached the FJ Cruiser, the dog, Lotte, poked her nose out of the window and gave a low bark. Sophie stumbled back, but Rand caught her, his hands on her shoulders steadying her. "Don't be afraid," he said. "She's just saying hello."

"How do you know? Maybe she doesn't like me."

"Dogs are like people. If you know what to look for, you can read their emotions." He gave her a gentle push. "Go on, get in the car. You two need to get used to each other."

"Why do we need to get used to each other?" she asked, but she made her way to the passenger side of the vehicle, keeping her gaze fixed on the dog. But Lotte ignored her, her attention focused on Rand.

"Lotte and I are a team." He slid into the driver's seat. "She's with me most of the day, and she goes home with me at night."

"She lives with you?" Sophie had thought the dog would stay in a kennel at headquarters when she wasn't working.

"Of course. She's my partner and I have to take care of her. Did you know that she outranks me?"

"What do you mean?"

"She's a sergeant. I'm only a corporal." He showed her the badge clipped to the dog's harness. "They do that on purpose, so the handler is sure to respect the dog. Not that I wouldn't respect Lotte." He scratched the dog behind the ears. She gazed up at him adoringly, mouth open to reveal a lot of gleaming, sharp teeth. Sophie took a step back, her heart racing.

"You sure you don't want to pet her?" Rand asked. "It might help you to see her as a friend."

Sophie shook her head. "I couldn't."

He shrugged, and closed the gate that blocked the dog from the front seat. Only then did Sophie get into the vehicle. "I know you think I'm silly," she said. "Fearing something you love so much."

"Fear isn't always rational," he said. "I get that. But I'd like to help you get over your fear, if I could."

"It might be easier if I started with a smaller dog," she said. "They look less frightening."

"Smaller dogs are more unpredictable than a trained working dog like Lotte."

"Yes, but if a toy poodle bites something, it's less likely to do damage."

"I guess there is that. What do you feel like eating?"

"Anything." She hadn't had much of an appetite since Lauren had disappeared.

They ended up at a Mexican food place not far from her hotel; Lotte settled down in the vehicle to wait while Rand and Sophie went inside. They ordered chips and salsa and enchiladas. She drank a margarita, while he stuck to iced tea. She tried not to be obvious as she studied him across the table.

"Do I pass inspection?" he asked.

She flushed. "You pass." He wasn't movie-star handsome—he needed a haircut and his nose had been broken once, probably a long time ago. She guessed he was a few years older than her— old enough to have the beginnings of fine lines around his eyes. He had the lean, muscular build of an athlete, and an air of competence that probably put most people at ease. She tried to come up with an adjective she would use to describe him to Lauren, but the word that filled her head was *sexy*.

Oh yeah, he was sexy, all right. Forget the badge and the gun and his position of authority. The real reason Rand made her nervous was that he made her feel more like a woman than she had felt in a long time. She wasn't merely a sister or an employee or a neighbor. She was a desirable female who'd been alone too long. Being with Rand made her lose her focus on her mission to find her sister. She forced her mind away from such dangerous thoughts and searched for some safe subject of conversation. "Emma told me you play lacrosse," she said.

"Yeah, I got into it in high school."

"What do you like about it?"

"It's a fast, physical game that requires strength, agility and real skill." He crunched a tortilla chip. "Plus, it's just fun. What do you like to do for fun?"

She forced herself not to squirm in her chair. She hated questions like this, because the answer made her sound so lame. "I like going out with friends and reading. That probably seems boring to you, I know..."

"No, I like those things, too."

The warmth of his smile made her want to cuddle up next to him. She traced one finger around the rim of her margarita glass. "Why are we here, having dinner together? Did the captain tell you to keep an eye on me?"

"No. I'm here because I want to be."

"Why? Do you think I'm guilty of something? Or do you feel sorry for me?" She had trouble getting the last words out. The last thing she wanted from him was pity.

He leaned toward her and took her hand. "I'm here because I like you and I want to be with you. I think you're a special woman and I want to get to know you better." He brushed his thumb across her knuckles, and a hot tremor passed through her, the heat settling low in her abdomen. She forced herself to meet his gaze, and the desire she found there shook her. Her instinct was to pull away, to run from that kind of intimacy.

He tightened his grip on her hand. "You don't have to be afraid of me," he said.

She ducked her head but didn't pull away, enjoying the warmth of his hand around hers. Enjoying the connection. "I'm not afraid," she said. A little nervous. Attracted. Aroused, even.

"I really like you," he said.

"Too bad we didn't meet under better circumstances." She reluctantly withdrew her hand.

"Do you believe if you don't think about your sister every minute it's going to make a difference?"

"The longer a person stays missing, the less likely there is to be a positive outcome—isn't that what they say?"

"That's generally true, yes."

"Then I feel guilty even sitting here having dinner. We should be out looking for her 24/7 until we find her."

"Random searches aren't very effective. You have to rest and regroup and focus on the most likely locations."

"Then why aren't you searching Richard Prentice's ranch?"

"Believe me, I'd like to go in there and tear the place apart. But we need to build a strong case against him. What if he's innocent?"

"If he's innocent, where is Lauren? Why haven't I heard from her?"

"Try to hold on to the fact that we haven't seen a single indicator of foul play or violence in this case," he said.

They hadn't seen anything, but that didn't mean Lauren hadn't been hurt, or even killed. She pressed her lips tightly together, determined not to break down in front of him. "I think I want to go back to the hotel now," she said. "I'm lousy company and I'm tired."

"Sure." He signaled the waitress to bring their check. She reached for her purse, but he waved her away. "I'll get this."

She said nothing else until he pulled to a stop in front of her hotel room. "Thank you for dinner," she said, fumbling with the seat belt.

"I'll walk you to your door." He came around to her side of the car, then walked with her up the outside stairs to her room. She kept her head down, lost in a fog of worry, but his hand, pulling her to him, brought her to full awareness again. "The door to your room is open," he said softly.

She stared dumbly at the door, which stood open about four inches. "I'm sure I locked it when I left," she said. "Maybe the maid…"

"Wait here." He drew the gun from his holster and approached the room, staying close to the wall. He stopped to listen for a moment, then nudged the door open with his foot. Nothing happened, so after another pause, he entered, gun at the ready. After another few seconds light spilled onto the walkway and he said, "It's okay for you to come in now. Don't touch anything."

She froze just inside the door, heart pounding, not comprehending the scene that lay before her, jagged images registering in her mind, like the reflection in a broken mirror—upended suitcase, covers dragged from the bed to pool on the floor, gray-white stuffing from the slashed pillows spilling across the top of the dresser, dresser drawers smashed and piled in one corner. Her gaze shifted to the mirror over the sink in the little dressing area outside the bathroom. Greasy pink letters a foot high and slanting upward spelled out STAY AWAY IF YOU WANT TO STAY ALIVE.

Chapter Ten

The room tipped and wobbled, and gray clouds rushed to swallow Sophie. Then Rand's arm was around her, supporting her as he led her to the bed and gently pushed her down to sit on the edge of the bare mattress. "Put your head between your knees," he said, pressing on her back until she bent forward and did as he commanded. "Now breathe in, deeply, not too fast. You're going to be all right."

She gripped his hand, aware of how icy she felt, all over. "Who did this?" she asked when she was able to sit upright and breathe again. She kept her eyes fixed on his, avoiding looking at the violence that had been wrought on the room around her.

"I don't know, but we'll find out." He continued to hold her hand, worry making him look older, as if she was glimpsing the man he'd be ten years from now. The idea reassured her, somehow. "Are you all right?" he asked.

She nodded and sat up straighter, forcing herself to release her grip on his hand, though as soon as they broke contact she felt bereft, and colder still. "Why would someone do this...to me?"

He shook his head. "Do you want to wait in the car until the local cops get here?"

"Will you wait with me?"

"Yes."

He led her outside, leaving the door open a few inches, the way they had found it. Lotte whined when Rand slid into the driver's seat, and pressed her nose against the grill. "She knows something's up," he said, and scratched her through the grate. "She wants to get out and go to work."

"Would she be able to track whoever did this?" Sophie forced herself to look at the dog, at the powerful muscles of her legs and shoulders, and the alert, forward tilt of her velvety ears. She was a beautiful animal, one likely to strike fear in the heart of anyone she turned against.

Sophie faced forward once more. Lotte wasn't turned against her. Rand wouldn't let the dog hurt her. She had to remember that.

They heard the police getting closer, sirens wailing. Two black-and-whites sped into the motel lot, one behind the other, and skidded to a halt behind Rand's SUV. Rand opened his door.

"I'm going to talk to them, but they'll probably have questions for you, too."

She nodded. "Sure."

The four officers—a woman, two white men and a black man—stood in a huddle outside the door, talking with Rand. Occasionally one of the men glanced her way, but too briefly for her to read his expression. After a moment, all five of them went into the room, where they stayed for what seemed like a long while.

Lotte panted softly, and Sophie sensed the dog's attention focused on the open room door, as well. Was this because Rand was inside, or because Lotte sensed that violence had taken place in there, the kind of violence she was trained to stop?

After half an hour or more, the female officer emerged from the room and walked over to Sophie's side of the vehicle. "Ms. Montgomery? I'm Officer Cagle, with the Montrose Police Department. I need to ask you a few questions."

"Of course." She glanced toward the room, wishing Rand would join them. But that was silly, she silently scolded herself. She was a grown woman, and she didn't have any reason to be afraid of Officer Cagle.

The questions were ordinary and expected: her basic information, why she was in Montrose, what she'd done that day. Officer Cagle made no comment on the fact that she'd had dinner with Rand. "Do you know of anyone—here or back home in Wisconsin—who might want to do something like this?" the officer asked. "A former boyfriend with a grudge? A coworker who is unhappy with you? A stalker?"

"No one." She shook her head emphatically. "I lead a very quiet life. I'm not the kind of person who makes enemies."

"What about the message on the mirror—'stay away if you want to stay alive'? What do you make of that?"

She wet her dry lips, fighting back the fear. "I…I came to town to look for my missing sister. Maybe…maybe someone who has something to do with her disappearance has heard I'm here and…and they don't like it?"

"Any names?"

Richard Prentice? But why would a billionaire even bother with someone like her? Phil Starling? But wasn't he in jail? She shook her head. "I don't know. It just seems so…so random."

Officer Cagle slipped her notebook into her pocket and straightened. "If you think of anything, let us know." She handed over a card. "That's my number, and of course, Officer Knightbridge can put you in touch with us. We're going to need to seal off the room until our investigation is complete, but if you like, you can come in and collect a few personal belongings—just what you'll need for the next day or so."

She nodded, and followed the officer into the room, stepping gingerly around an officer who was photographing the scene, then skirting debris from the rampage to arrive at the bathroom. She collected her makeup bag—minus the tube of rose-pink lipstick she'd bought only the week before, and which now lay broken in the sink. She kneeled in front of the upended suitcase and reached for a pair of underwear, then snatched back her hand as if she'd been slapped and let out a small cry.

"What is it?" Officer Cagle kneeled beside Sophie.

"My clothes...the underwear..." She choked back another cry and pointed a wavering finger at the pile of garments.

With the tip of a pen, Officer Cagle picked up the pair of underwear on top. It was slashed through the middle of the crotch, neatly sliced through satin and cotton. The other clothes were similarly cut, very precisely across the portions of the fabric that would have covered her most intimate parts.

Sophie turned away, feeling sick.

"It's okay. You're going to be all right." Rand's

voice, soft in her ear. His arms, strong around her, lifting her. "Come with me."

He led her outside, into the fresh air. She breathed in deep gulps, as if the oxygen could somehow wash away the image of her violated wardrobe. Rand continued to hold her close, until at last her trembling subsided. "I know this feels really personal," he said. "Whoever did this wants you to feel that way. They're playing a psychological game. But you're stronger than they are. You're not going to let them defeat you."

"I don't feel strong."

"You are strong. A weak woman wouldn't have come all this way to help her sister. A weak woman wouldn't have stood up to me and the rest of the Rangers and demanded we help you."

"Then I guess I've used up all my courage on those things. I don't feel like I have any left."

"You just need time to regroup and let it build back up." He took his arm from around her shoulders, but kept his hand resting lightly at her back. "Are you ready to go?"

"Go where?"

"Back to my place. You can rest, and I know you'll be safe there."

She hesitated. "What about my car?"

"I'll have an officer drive it over."

She couldn't impose on him that way. He

couldn't assume what was best for her. They didn't have that kind of relationship… She opened her mouth to refuse.

What came out was "Thank you. I'll feel much safer there." In truth, she couldn't think of anywhere she'd rather be right now than with Rand Knightbridge.

RAND DIDN'T SAY anything on the drive back to his duplex. If Sophie didn't feel like talking, he wasn't going to force her. But he kept glancing at her still figure belted into the passenger seat, her face chalky white. Would it be better if she broke down and cried? Maybe releasing her emotions would be more beneficial than this distant, terrifying calm. He gripped the steering wheel so tightly his knuckles ached as he fought a rage against whoever had done this to her. He'd tried to make light of the seriousness of the attack, not wanting to worry her, but the discovery of her slashed underwear and clothing had sent a chill clear through him. They weren't dealing with some random punk out to make trouble. Whoever was responsible for this attack had a hatred of women in general—or of Sophie in particular—that could lead to further violence.

All the more reason to keep Sophie as close as possible, where he could ensure her safety. "Here we are, home, sweet home." He forced a relaxed cheerfulness into his voice that he didn't feel as they pulled into the driveway of the duplex. A quick check of the area revealed nothing out of the ordinary. Marco's half of the driveway was empty; Rand had called and asked him to check in with the Montrose cops, to see what they turned up. The other cars on the street were familiar to him, and lights shone in the neighbors' houses, the yellow of lamplight and the blue glow of televisions.

He let Lotte out of the back of the SUV and she trotted ahead of them into the house. Rand and Sophie followed. Rand flipped on all the lights and led the way toward the kitchen, pausing to kick dirty socks under the sofa and to close an open cabinet door. "Can I get you some coffee or tea, or maybe a drink?" he asked.

"Don't go to any trouble." She looked around her, and he was conscious of the dirty dishes in the sink and the takeout pizza box protruding from the top of the trash can.

"Sorry it's a little messy," he said.

"You don't have to apologize. You weren't expecting company."

"Sit down." She looked ready to fall down. He pulled out a chair at the kitchen table.

She sat and he moved to a cupboard and rummaged around until he unearthed some herbal tea he'd bought in an attempt to self-treat a cold one time, along with honey from the same episode. Hot drinks with sugar—wasn't that what people said was good for shock? He set a pan of water to boil. He was debating what to do next when his phone rang.

"Hey, Marco," he answered. "What's up?"

"We're not getting much out of the hotel room," he said. "CSI is still trying to lift prints, but the perps probably wore gloves. Is Sophie sure nothing was taken?"

He turned to Sophie. "Marco wants to know if anything was taken from your hotel room."

She shook her head. "Nothing. I had my money and my phone with me. I didn't bring a laptop or anything like that. Do they really think this was a robbery attempt?"

"Tossing the suitcase and dresser indicates the perp was looking for something," Rand said. "If nothing is missing, he didn't find what he was looking for."

"I don't think it was robbery," Sophie said. "I think whoever it was wanted to frighten me. And I'd say he succeeded."

"I'm going to put Marco on speaker so you can hear him," Rand said. "Marco, did you get that about nothing missing?"

"Maybe the perp was looking for the photograph," Marco said. "The one of Milbanks and Prentice."

"But I turned that over to you guys," she said.

"Whoever did this may not know that," Rand said.

"What good would the photograph do anyone?" Sophie asked.

"It's the strongest link we have between Prentice and Milbanks," Rand said. It might be the link they needed to finally bring Prentice to justice.

"We're trying to bring Prentice in for questioning," Marco said. "His lawyers are stalling, but Graham hinted he could arrange for the photo to be leaked to the press. I think that's going to persuade them to be more cooperative."

"Let's hope so," Rand said. He said good-night and disconnected the call, but it vibrated again immediately.

"Don't put me on speaker," Marco said. "I don't want Sophie to hear."

"Okay." Rand turned his back and busied himself at the stove. "What's up?"

"One more thing you need to know," Marco said. "Phil Starling was released on bond this afternoon, about four o'clock."

"Gotcha." He hung up and finished making the tea for Sophie, his mind racing. If Phil was out of jail by four, he could easily have driven to Sophie's hotel and trashed her room while they were at dinner. Maybe his feelings for his former sister-in-law went deeper than mere disdain.

Rand fed Lotte her kibble. Sophie watched the dog eat, leaning as far away from the dish as possible without getting up from her chair. "Let's go in the other room," he said. "We'll be more comfortable in there."

He took her elbow and escorted her out of the room, keeping himself between her and the dog. He didn't completely understand her fear of Lotte, but he believed she wasn't faking it. They sat on the sofa, where she perched on the edge of the cushion, hands cupped around the mug of tea balanced on her knee.

"Relax. I won't bite." He kept his voice light, not letting on how much her distance hurt, after the closeness they'd shared not an hour before. Over dinner and even later, after they'd first discovered her trashed hotel room, he'd thought she was letting down her guard with him—enjoying his company, even.

She leaned back against the cushions, though tension still radiated from her.

"Would you like it better if I sat over there?" He motioned to the recliner across the room.

"No. No, this is fine." She sipped her tea, her gaze shifting around the room, looking at anything but him.

"Do you want me to put Lotte in the other

room?" The dog had finished eating and lay on a pad beside the recliner, head resting on her front paws.

"I...I'd forgotten she was even in the room."

"Then what is it?" He scooted forward to sit closer to her, almost—but not quite—touching her. "Don't you trust me?"

"I trust you." She swallowed and rubbed one hand, palm down, along the side of her thigh. "But I'm not sure I trust myself."

"What do you mean?" He tried to read her expression, but she wasn't giving off clear signals. Was she afraid? Angry? Guilty?

"I'm not the person you think I am," she said.

"How do you know what I think about you?"

"It's what everyone thinks about me—that I'm this quiet, plain, serious woman who never steps out of line. I'm responsible and sober and dependable and I never cause any trouble at all."

"Are you saying you have caused trouble?" he asked.

"More than you can imagine."

Chapter Eleven

Sophie waited for some reaction from Rand—shock, disbelief, even argument. But all he did was settle back against the cushions and regard her calmly. "Tell me about it," he said. "I'm not in any hurry. And some people say I'm a good listener."

She sipped the tea, which had grown cold. What would it hurt to tell him? Maybe it would help him understand the things that drove her. She set aside the half-empty mug and hugged a pillow to her chest. "When we were girls, Lauren was always into mischief," she began. "She wasn't a bad child, just more daring than I was, more likely to bend the rules."

Lauren had been beautiful and winsome, even as a toddler, all blond curls and blue eyes and perfect dimples. "She was an angel child, with the personality of an imp," she continued. "Lauren was the one who climbed to the top of the playground gym and jumped off into a mud puddle, or who decided, when she was seven, that she wanted to drive the car and backed it into a tree. She ran away from home when she was thirteen, and again when she was fifteen. She dated the wildest boys, racked up traffic tickets and curfew violations, got caught skipping school and smoking pot and drinking when she was underage. Our parents dragged her to therapists and summer school and extracurricular activities, in a vain effort to curb an exuberance they didn't yet recognize as mania."

"And what were you doing while all this was going on?" Rand asked.

"I suppose to make up for all the trouble she caused, I tried to be better, more responsible," Sophie said. "I was like everyone else—I adored her and let her get away with things. No one could stay angry with her. She was so charming and witty, and really sweet. Not a malicious bone in her body. And maybe we all sensed, even then, that there was something different about her brain that made it impossible for her to fit into the mold everyone else had to conform to."

"How old was she before she was diagnosed with bipolar disorder?" Rand asked.

"Not until this year. Isn't that wild? But she did a good job of masking her worst symptoms, and after a while we all took it for granted that that was her personality. Whenever she did something a little off, we thought she was just being Lauren."

"While you were the good, responsible daughter," he said.

"Yes, but when I was a freshman in college, Lauren was still in high school, and she had the first of what I know now was a major manic episode. She lost control. She ran away and ended up in jail in a town just across the state line, charged with destruction of property and disturbing the peace." The horror of those days still made a knot in the pit of her stomach—hushed conversations between her parents, angry outbursts followed by tears, everyone tiptoeing around, fragile and furious and fearful. "My dad was able to pull strings and hush up the incident. The charges were dropped and Lauren came home and finished school in a private boarding facility. It cost my parents a lot of money—so much that they asked me to take a semester off college."

"Ouch!" Rand said. "That must have hurt."

"Oh, yes. I was furious—not just about having to postpone my schooling, but about all the attention Lauren had taken away from me for all those years. Instead of leaving school and coming home, as my parents asked me to do, I stayed and got a job working at a bar to pay my living expenses. I thought they only wanted me to come home to look after Lauren. They'd expect me to go with her everywhere, to be responsible for her so they didn't have to."

"Had they done that kind of thing before—made you her caretaker?"

"Yes. And I hated it. I wanted a normal sister, one I could have a normal relationship with. And I was tired of always being the responsible one. During that time, I hardly spoke to my parents, and I cut off any contact with Lauren."

"I think that's understandable," he said.

"No, it's not," she said. "I was being a brat. My poor parents. They were losing one daughter to mental illness, they'd practically bankrupted themselves and I was only making things worse with my little temper tantrum."

"You were what—nineteen?" he asked.

"I was. But I should have known better."

"If you say so. But living away from home when you're legally an adult isn't even a minor crime, much less anything you need to ashamed of."

"No, that's not the shameful part. I'm getting to that." She hugged the pillow to her chest and wished there'd been something stronger than honey in that tea. She could have used a bit of false courage to get through this next part. "While I was working at the bar, I met a man," she said. "He was older, a customer who came in fairly often. He was handsome and charming and I was really attracted to him—more than I'd ever been attracted to anyone before. I'd dated a little before then, but never anything serious, and all those guys seemed like boys compared to this man. He made me feel so special."

"You were starved for attention and he gave that to you."

She glanced at him, then away. She didn't know whether to be impressed or wary, that he could read her so well. "I guess that was it. But at the time I thought I was in love. We'd known each other only a couple of weeks when I moved in with him. I made a point of telling my parents, of course. They were devastated. I thought they were upset because I'd proved they could no longer control me."

"What happened with the guy?" He moved closer, his thigh brushing hers. She sensed the heat of him through the denim, and she fought the urge to lean into him.

"He stopped being so nice once we were living together," she said. "He took my money and accused me of cheating on him—though I found out later he had two other girlfriends. After three months with him I was broke and I'd lost my job at the bar because he'd threatened my boss. I didn't have any choice but to go home to my parents."

"How did they react to that?"

"They seemed thrilled. It was more relief than anything, I suspect. By that time, Lauren had calmed down and I think they were happy to have both of us back under their roof and seemingly stable. But they'd aged terribly in the few months I'd been away—graying hair and sagging skin. I saw what my running away—and that's what I'd done, really, run away—had done to them." She swallowed past the hard knot in her throat that was equal parts unshed tears and an unuttered primal scream, and forced herself to go on. "I hadn't been home even a week when they were both killed in a car accident."

Only the dog's soft snores and the low growl of a big rig out on the highway disturbed the silence that stretched between them. Rand cleared his throat. "Do you really think I'm like that man?" he asked. "The one who used you?"

"No. I'm sure you're not." She turned toward him, her knees bumping into his. This was the scariest part yet, the words she almost couldn't say. "I…I'm attracted to you the same way I was attracted to him," she said. "And I'm not sure of my motives. Are the things I feel when I'm around you real, or are they just because I resent having to once again upset my whole life because of something Lauren did? Am I trying to declare my independence from the needs of my family in the only way I know how?" Articulating these questions only raised more doubts; she'd had so little experience relating to men on anything but the most casual terms since that college disaster that she had no idea what it was like to feel a normal attraction to someone.

"You were a kid then," he said. "The fact that you're even thinking about this shows you've learned a few things."

"I would hope so, but I don't know." She smoothed both hands down her thighs, her palms clammy. "I just...I don't trust myself anymore. Especially with everything in such turmoil with Lauren's disappearance."

"Maybe you're overthinking this." He took one of her hands in his, cradling it between his palms. "Why can't we just be two people who enjoy each other's company, without any expectations?"

"There can't be any expectations." She tried to pull her hand away, but he wouldn't let her. "I'm only going to be here a little while," she said. "Until we find Lauren."

"Then you'll go back to Madison." He kept his voice even, stating a fact.

"Yes...at least I will, unless Lauren needs me." She hadn't even realized the truth of these words until now. Whatever happened, she wouldn't desert her sister.

"You've always been there for her," he said.

"She's my sister. And the only family I have left."

"I hope she knows how lucky she is to have you. But maybe it's time someone was here for you." He leaned closer, and ducked his head to press his lips against hers.

She stilled, startled by the suddenness of the gesture, yet aware that she'd been waiting for it—wanting it—ever since he'd sat beside her on the sofa. He squeezed her hand, a gesture of reassurance, and increased the pressure of his lips slightly. She relaxed, and as the warmth of his nearness engulfed her, she melted against him, sliding her free hand up his chest and over his shoulder to cradle his head in her palm and draw him closer still.

He tilted his head to achieve a better angle and coaxed her lips apart. She opened to him eagerly, almost desperately, pressing against him, nipples beading against the hard wall of his chest. The sweep of his tongue inside her mouth sent little shock waves of pleasure through her that reverberated all the way to her toes. Desire, hot and urgent, flooded her, making her clutch at him when at last he pulled away.

They stared at each other, openmouthed, breath coming in ragged gasps, his gaze a little unfocused, as she was sure hers was. "That was…intense," he said, his voice rough, like sandpaper across sensitive nerve endings.

"Yeah." All she could manage was a whisper. She stared at his lips, wanting him to kiss her again, wondering if she had the nerve to insist on it.

He did kiss her again, more gently, a tender exploration of lips and tongue that was just as dizzying, if less urgent. She rested her palm flat between them, not pushing him away, but keeping herself a little apart from him, trying to keep her wits about her. But it was like trying to fight the tide, the pull of him relentless and so strong…

She was the first to pull away this time, withdrawing her hands and looking away, not wanting him to read the turmoil of her emotions reflected in her eyes. "I don't think I'm very good at this relationship stuff," she said. The best they could hope for, given her circumstances, was a casual affair. A temporary fling. But nothing about her feelings for him felt casual or temporary.

"I don't want to rush you," he said.

No. She was the one who wanted to rush—headlong into the kind of emotional minefield she'd spent years avoiding. She didn't even know herself anymore when she was this close to him.

He stood. "You look exhausted," he said. "Let

me show you to the bedroom. You can sleep in one of my old T-shirts, if you want." At her startled look, he chuckled. "Don't worry, I'll sleep on the sofa."

"I feel bad, taking your bed," she said as she followed him to the bedroom.

"It's okay." He left her at the door with a light kiss on the cheek. "Good night. Sleep well."

He sauntered down the hall, humming softly under his breath. She closed the door and leaned against it, eyes squeezed shut and forehead pressed against the wood. She could still feel his lips on hers, the firm curve of his muscular chest, the grip of his hand in hers. He could give her his bed, but she didn't expect she'd sleep much in it, knowing he was spending the night only a few feet away.

SOPHIE WOKE TO BARKING—sharp, percussive explosions of sound that sent panic spiraling up from her stomach to constrict her chest. She sat up and blinked at the gray light filtering behind the blinds. Nothing in the room looked familiar, yet it clearly wasn't a hotel room.

"Lotte, silence!"

The quiet but commanding voice calmed her as well as the dog, and she remembered she was in Rand Knightbridge's duplex—in his bedroom. She eased back down into sheets that carried the faint scent of his cologne. Lying here alone, listening to him and his dog move about, made her feel that much more isolated. Despite her fears to the contrary, exhaustion had overcome anxiety and within minutes of climbing into bed she'd succumbed to a deep, dreamless sleep. But the escape felt like just that—a fleeing from the consequences of the previous night's events.

What would have happened if she'd asked him to spend the night with her in this bed, instead of sending him to sleep on the sofa? Would things have been awkward between them this morning, or would she have felt more sure of herself, better prepared to face the events of the day?

He tapped on the door. "Sophie? Are you awake?"

She sat up again and pulled the covers up to her neck. "I'm awake," she called.

The door eased open and his face filled the gap. His hair was tousled and he hadn't yet shaved—probably because all his things were in here with her. "Want some coffee?" he asked.

"That would be great."

"If you want, you can grab the shower while I make the coffee.

"Sure. What time is it?" She looked around for a clock.

"Early. Just a little after six."

"Do you always get up this early?"

He grimaced. "Only when I have to. But the captain called and wants us all at the station early."

"Why? Has something happened?" She sat up straighter, more alert.

"I'll tell you at breakfast. See you in a minute." He shut the door before she could question him more.

In the bathroom, she examined Rand's shampoo, toothpaste and soap, noting they preferred the same brand of toothpaste. What did a man's choice of toiletries say about him? Rand's seemed to say that he was an uncomplicated man who stuck to basics. He was well-groomed, but not vain. A woman wouldn't have to compete with him for space in the medicine cabinet.

She showered quickly, resisting the urge to luxuriate in the flow of hot water, then dressed and dried her hair. Only light makeup this morning—a touch of lip gloss and a sweep of mascara would have to do, since she didn't want to keep Rand waiting.

He sat at the table in the kitchen, hunched over a bowl of cereal. "The coffee's ready," he said. "For breakfast, there's toast or cereal. Sorry, but I'm not much of a cook."

"That's okay." She poured coffee into the mug he'd set beside the machine, and sat at the table across from him. "Why do you have to go into the office early?" she asked.

"I'm probably not supposed to tell you."

"Is it something to do with Lauren?" Her hand trembled as she set down her coffee mug. Had they found her sister—or only her body?

"Maybe not."

Which meant that maybe it did. "Then what is it? Don't keep me in suspense like this," she pleaded.

"We're bringing in Richard Prentice for questioning."

Him again? Did a man with everything in the world going for him really have something to do with Lauren's disappearance, much less the other crimes the Rangers seemed to think him guilty of? "Do you think he knows something about Lauren?"

"We don't know, though I'm sure the captain will be asking those questions." He stood and carried his empty cereal bowl to the sink. "I probably won't be in on the questioning."

"What prompted this? Did the investigators find something in my hotel room that pointed to Prentice?"

"No. But the picture you found links him to Alan Milbanks. We want to question him about that, and about Milbanks's drug-dealing activities, and anything else we can link him to."

"When will this happen?"

"Soon. I have to be at headquarters by seven. I imagine we'll pick him up after that."

"Will he even be awake?"

"All the better if he isn't. Pulling people out of bed is a good way to catch them off guard. And we want to do this before his lawyers are in the office."

"Why?"

"Not because we want to violate his rights, but because lawyers always throw up roadblocks. They'd make it impossible for us to question him at all, even if the answers might completely clear him from suspicion."

"Do you think the photograph of Preston and Milbanks together is what the people who trashed my hotel room were looking for?" she asked.

"Maybe. If they didn't know you'd already turned the picture over to us. Or maybe they only wanted to frighten you."

"They did a good job of that." She hugged her arms across her chest and shivered.

He squeezed her shoulder. "I know it's hard, but hang in there."

"What will I do while you're with Prentice and the other Rangers?" she asked.

"You can stay here. The place has an alarm system. You'll be safe."

More waiting and not knowing what was happening. She didn't know if she could stand it. "What will you do while Prentice is being questioned? Will you search his house?"

"We can't do that without a warrant. We're hoping we'll get something from the questioning that will convince a judge to grant the search warrant."

"His lawyers will try to keep that from happening."

"Yes, they will. But we'll push back as hard as we can. They can't fight us forever." He dropped his hand from her shoulder. "I'm going to take my shower. Don't worry about the dishes. I'll do them when I come home."

He left the house while she was still sitting at the kitchen table, drinking coffee. She wandered into the living room and turned on the television, then turned it off again. She wasn't going to do this. She wasn't going to sit and let others do all the work of looking for her sister. Maybe the police had to wait for a warrant in order to search Richard Prentice's house, but she didn't have to. Now, while she knew he was away, was the best time to find out if Lauren was locked away in some room of that mansion.

She grabbed her keys and hurried to the rental car, and the malaise that had dragged at her vanished. If she got caught in Prentice's house, she'd be in trouble, but she'd make sure she didn't get caught. She'd always been a quiet person, the kind other people didn't notice. She could use that to her advantage now.

Chapter Twelve

Sophie consulted the map in her car and figured out the route to Prentice's ranch. On the drive over, she debated how to deal with the guards at the gate. They'd never let her in, so her best bet was to ditch the car somewhere and hike in, avoiding the guards. She stopped at a convenience store and bought a bottle of water and some energy bars. She wished she had a weapon, then discarded the idea. Her cell phone would be her best weapon. At the first sign of trouble she'd call Rand and alert him.

She drove past the ranch and parked the car behind a telephone-relay building a quarter mile past the gate. It wasn't completely invisible from the road, but she figured someone would have to be specifically looking for her in order to notice the vehicle. With luck, she'd be back to the car before anyone became suspicious.

She hurried along the road, planning to hide behind a tree or dive into the ditch if anyone drove past, but no one did. When she came to the wood rail fence that marked Prentice's property line, she checked the area for security cameras and, seeing none, ducked between the rails and headed across the prairie in the direction she thought the house was situated.

Before long she could make out the narrow gravel drive that led to the mansion. She kept to the field to the left of it. Dressed in faded jeans and a brown-and-tan blouse, she hoped she blended in with the landscape of drying grasses, cacti and shrubby trees. She wondered what Abby Stewart had found to study in these surroundings. This wasn't exactly desert, but it was close.

The house appeared on the horizon, a gray hulk that looked out of place against the backdrop of distant mountains and turquoise sky, like a Scottish castle set down on the surface of the moon. She stopped to drink some water and study the building, wondering if she should approach from the back.

A cloud of dust rose in the distance, lifting up from the ground in a soft white fog and hovering near the horizon. Then the cloud grew larger... closer. With a start, she realized a car was approaching, barreling down the unpaved road toward her.

She dropped to the ground, flattening herself in the dirt, ignoring the bite of sharp stones into her knees and the tangle of sticks in her hair. She stared at the approaching cloud, too frightened to draw more than shallow breaths.

Then tension eased as she realized the car was headed away from the house, and the two men inside, dressed in brown camouflage fatigues, didn't appear to have noticed her. She wished she had binoculars so she could get a better look at them. Were they leaving, or merely on patrol?

She lay in the grass a long time after they left, shifting after a while to pull out her phone to check the time. If the Rangers had met with Prentice at their headquarters at, say, half past seven at the earliest, the interview had only just begun. She had plenty of time to get up to the house and away again before he was due to return home. All she had to do was find the right opportunity to get closer and seize it.

When the Jeep didn't return after fifteen minutes, she decided it was safe to proceed. She crossed the gravel drive and circled the house, keeping low and avoiding any cameras she saw. She counted two in the front of the house and one in the rear. She decided that if she stayed close to the wall of the house, she'd be out of view of the camera at the rear.

She crept along the side of the house, the rough stone catching and pulling at her clothes. After waiting and listening ten minutes and hearing and seeing nothing and no one, she hurried up the steps and tried the back door, stopping first to wrap her hand in the tail of her shirt. Why hadn't she bothered to bring gloves?

She gasped when the knob turned easily in her hand. Holding her breath, she pushed it open and waited for the blare of an alarm. But maybe that wasn't how security systems worked. Rand had showed her how to punch in the code to his system, but he hadn't told her what would happen if she failed to do so. Maybe the system sent a silent alarm to the police, or to a private security company.

But she hadn't come this far to turn back now, especially because of something she wasn't even sure would happen. Richard Prentice had so many of his own guards and cameras on this place, why would he need to pay for an alarm? Resolute, she slipped into the house, and shut the door softly behind her.

She found herself standing in a mudroom that was larger than her bedroom back in Madison. Through an open doorway she spotted the kitchen, gleaming with marble and stainless steel. A quick check showed this room to be empty, as pristine and undisturbed as a kitchen in a model home, where no one lived or ever cooked.

Walking lightly, one foot placed carefully in

front of the other, she traversed the kitchen, a formal dining room and a hallway. The first door she tried in the hallway was locked. She debated trying to open it, but unlike the heroines in television crime dramas, she had no idea how to go about doing so.

She moved on to the stairs. The risers were covered with an Oriental patterned runner, but every so often one let out a creak that sounded as loud as a firecracker in her ears. She stopped at the top of the landing, listening, but the house held the silence and stillness of an unoccupied dwelling.

Staying close to the wall, she moved down the hall, peeking into the open doors that lined the passage: a game room with a pool table and a dartboard that looked as if they'd never been used, a home gym with free weights, a treadmill and a complicated-looking exercise machine with bands and bars and a digital readout. She did a cursory tour through these, then moved on to the end of the hall and an unoccupied bedroom.

This room was furnished with a massive fourposter bed and dresser that both looked antique, but she suspected were expensive reproductions. Layers of silky drapes shrouded the window, over which a black-out shade was drawn. Half a dozen pillows almost obscured the carved headboard, and a check under the brocade comforter revealed sheets heavily trimmed with cotton lace. Did that mean someone was using this room? Or that guests were expected very soon?

Under the bed she found nothing but dust bunnies, though were those smudges an indication that someone had stood at the edge of the bed, perhaps before climbing in for the night? She moved on to the adjoining bathroom, which gleamed with marble basins and pewter fixtures, the beveled mirror reflecting a tiled steam shower big enough for two. She traced the outline on the counter where a trio of bottles had recently sat. Shampoo? Perfume? Lotion? And who did these things belong to? It wasn't as if Richard Prentice would use this room himself, or any of his guards. As far as she knew, from her own visit and information she'd gleaned from listening to the Rangers talk about the billionaire, he lived in the house alone.

Still puzzling over this, she opened the door to the shower. Fragrant humidity hit her in the face, the smell of lavender and vanilla, a soft, feminine fragrance. A tickle of apprehension danced up her spine. Did Richard Prentice have a girlfriend staying with him? A female relative?

She returned to the bedroom, in time to hear the scrape of metal on wood, like a door slamming. She froze in place as heavy footsteps crossed the downstairs rooms, then started up the stairs.

When whoever it was reached the top of the stairs, Sophie looked around frantically for somewhere to hide. She started for the bed, thinking to dive under, then whirled and dove into the closet instead. She closed the door with a soft click seconds before the footsteps turned into the room.

Choking back a gasp, she pressed her ear to the door, but all she could hear was the thudding of her own frantic pulse. What was going on out there? She didn't dare open the door to look, and no old-fashioned keyhole afforded a peek into the room. The narrow gap at the bottom of the door let in a dim light, but there was no way could she stretch out enough in this small space to look through.

As her eyes adjusted to the darkness, she could make out clothes filling the bar across the back of the closet, with various boxes and bags sitting along the shelf above. But before she could investigate any of these, the bedsprings creaked loudly. What was he doing? She prayed he hadn't decided to take a nap. Maybe she'd been wrong about the room's occupant. Maybe it wasn't a woman at all. She thought the person out there must be male, given the heaviness of his tread.

She needed a weapon. The kind of thing

someone might keep in a closet—a baseball bat? Golf club? Dropping into a crouch, she felt along the back wall, then the sides, then the floor. She came up with a shoe—a woman's dark stiletto. It didn't have the weight or heft of a club or bat, but if whoever was out there opened the door, she'd hit him as hard as she could, driving the pointed heel into his face. It would hurt like hell, and maybe give her enough time to get away.

The bed creaked again, and then the footsteps retreated—across the room, down the hall, on the stairs, all the way out the door, which closed with the solid click of the lock catching. Sophie closed her eyes and sagged against the wall, too afraid to give in much to relief. Maybe whoever had been out there had discovered something to make him suspicious and had merely gone for help. She had to get out of here while she still could.

She peered out the door, making sure the coast was clear. The only sign that she hadn't imagined the last ten minutes was the rumpled comforter and the faint impression on the mattress, as if someone heavy had lain there for a short while.

She was halfway across the room before she realized she was still holding the shoe. She couldn't leave it out here, and carrying it across the prairie would be awkward. In the full light, it didn't look like much of a weapon, the heel a thin column wrapped in leather, the upper a network of leather straps, a bow at the instep. The insole bore the name of a designer Sophie recognized as expensive. Lauren had owned several pairs of that particular brand. In fact, she would have loved this shoe. Sophie checked the label again; yes, it was just Lauren's size.

She hurried back to the closet and flicked on the light. More shoes filled boxes on the top shelf, all styles Lauren would have loved, in her favorite brands and her size. She turned her attention to the clothes—a beaded evening gown in the royal blue Lauren favored, also in her size. Sophie pressed her face against the fabric and inhaled deeply. The scent of Mitsouko permeated the silk. The desire to shout for joy warred with the urge to weep. Instead of doing either, she released her hold on the dress and turned her attention to the woman's purse on the shelf. The bag proved to be empty. Disappointed, she started to close it again, then spotted a slip of cardboard peeking out of a small pocket sewn into one side of the lining. She pinched the cardboard between thumb and forefinger and teased it out. *Lauren Starling* was printed in crisp black lettering beneath the image of a stylized bird.

RICHARD PRENTICE WASN'T happy to be at the police station and he let everyone know it. He didn't raise his voice, but his tone was scathing. His lawyers—two of them—were equally imperious. "Keep that beast away from me," one snarled as he followed his client down the hallway, glaring at Lotte, who sat at Rand's side, attention fixed on the new arrivals, with their expensive suits and haughty airs.

"The dog doesn't intimidate me," Prentice said. He strode past Rand and Lotte without a second glance, into the interrogation room, with its gray walls and utilitarian table and chairs. "Let's get this over with. I don't intend for you to waste any more of my time than is absolutely necessary."

They'd chosen not to question him at Ranger headquarters, but at the Montrose police station, which had a proper interrogation room, with recording equipment and cameras. Rand and Marco watched from another room while the captain and Lieutenant Michael Dance handled the questioning.

"Earlier you told us you didn't know Lauren Starling," Graham began, after logging the preliminary information of Prentice's name, address and the date and time. "But you told her sister the two of you were friends. Such good friends that Ms. Starling confided to you her worries about her job."

"That's hearsay," one of the lawyers interjected.

"We're not in court here, counselor." Graham kept his attention focused on Prentice. "Answer the question."

"My friends are none of the government's business." Prentice's tone was clipped, as if he couldn't be bothered wasting breath on their concerns.

"They are when one of the friends has been missing for over a month and you may be the only person she knew here," Michael said.

"You're merely speculating," Prentice said, even before his lawyers could interrupt. "A woman like Lauren Starling, who works in the public arena, knows many people."

"Then you tell us," Graham said. "What was she doing in Montrose?"

"I have no idea."

"She didn't stop by to say hello while she was here?" Michael asked.

"She did not."

"When was the last time you saw her?" Michael continued the questioning, while Graham stood, arms folded, leaning against the wall, glowering at Prentice.

"I haven't seen Lauren for some time. Several months at least."

"How many months?"

"I don't know. It was at a charity function. I can have my secretary research my calendar and get back to you."

"You do that." Michael's voice held a sour note. "When was the last time you talked to her?"

"I don't remember."

"We can subpoena your phone records and find out," Graham said.

"Then maybe you should do that." Tone defiant, eyes hard as stones.

"Are you giving us permission to do so?" Graham asked.

"He is not!" The older of the two lawyers spoke.

"I am not," Prentice agreed.

"This is getting nowhere," Rand said.

"They haven't asked him about Alan Milbanks yet," Marco said.

"What is your relationship with Alan Milbanks?" Graham asked.

"Who?" Prentice looked blank.

Michael slid a piece of paper across the table—Rand assumed it was the photograph.

Prentice studied the image without expression. "Who is that?" he asked.

"It's a picture of you and Alan Milbanks," Rand said.

Prentice leaned over the picture, studying it closely. "I don't know who that is in the picture. It's not me."

"Do you have a twin?" Michael asked.

Prentice merely glared.

"He's a cold one," Rand said. "How can he look the captain in the eye and deny that's him in the photo?"

"Lying is like anything else," Marco said. "You get better with practice."

"Then I'd say Prentice has had a lot of practice," Rand said.

"That is a dark, blurry photo of someone who vaguely resembles my client," the older lawyer said. "My client has already denied it is him, and you have no proof that it is."

"This picture shows a meeting between you and Alan Milbanks." Michael stabbed a finger at the picture. "A known drug dealer who is now dead."

"I don't know anyone named Milbanks and I certainly don't know anything about his death."

"It's interesting to me that people you associate with keep dying." Michael pulled out a chair and sat next to Prentice. "First your pilot, Bobby Pace, and now your friend Milbanks."

"We're done here, gentlemen." The older lawyer stood and the other lawyer and Prentice rose also.

Marco checked his watch. "Twenty minutes. That's longer than I thought we'd get."

"Twenty minutes wasted," Rand said.

"Not necessarily. We showed our hand. Now we see if we made him nervous enough to do something stupid."

"Or maybe this just gives his lawyers more ammunition. We'll get to read in the papers tomorrow about our continued harassment of an innocent man."

They moved back into the hallway in time to see Prentice walking out, flanked by his lawyers. Lotte growled low, under her breath. Rand rubbed behind her ears. "That's right. You know the bad guys when you see them." They joined Graham and Michael in the interrogation room. "What do you think?" Rand asked.

"He's lying about Milbanks," Graham said. "His eyebrow twitches when he's stressed—it's a tell Emma clued me into. It was twitching like crazy when I showed him the photograph."

Rand hadn't picked up on that. "Anything when you asked about Lauren?"

Graham shook his head.

"So what now?" Michael asked.

"CSI towed Lauren's car this morning," Graham said. "They're going to go over it again and see if we turn up anything new. How's her sister?"

"The scene at her hotel room yesterday shook her up some, but she's hanging tough."

"Everything go okay last night?" Graham studied him intently.

"Fine." He'd tossed and turned most of the night, kept awake by the memory of those incredible kisses, torn between the desire to get up and knock on the bedroom door and invite himself in, and worry that she'd reject him. In the end, his responsibility to protect her and help her through this overcame his desire.

"Let her know we aren't giving up," Graham said.

"I will."

His phone rang. He checked the display and felt a catch in his chest. "It's Sophie. She's probably calling to ask how things went with Prentice. How much can I tell her?"

"Tell her we didn't learn anything new, but we're still working on it."

He punched the button to answer the call. "Hello, Sophie."

"Rand, you have to get out to Richard Prentice's ranch right away." She sounded out of breath, her voice an excited whisper.

"Why? What's going on?"

"I'm here now, in an upstairs bedroom. There's a closet with women's clothing and shoes, all in Lauren's size. The dresses smell of her perfume—I'm sure she's been wearing them. And I found a purse with one of her business cards in it."

"Sophie, what are you doing there?" Disbelief and alarm made him speak more loudly than he'd intended, drawing attention from the others.

"I knew he'd be at the station with you, so I thought this would be the perfect opportunity to look around."

"Sophie, you have to get out of there," Rand said, his agitation growing.

"I promise I was careful with everything."

"Sophie, get out of there now." He couldn't believe she was taking such a terrible risk. "Prentice is on his way back there."

"All right. But do you think this is enough to get a warrant to search the place? Lauren was here, I know it. She may still be here now."

"We'll talk about it when you're safe."

"Maybe I should look around a little longer."

"No!" He almost shouted the word. Taking a deep breath, he tried to calm down. "That isn't safe."

"All right, but… Okay. I have to go. Someone's coming."

"Sophie? Sophie?" The line went dead.

Chapter Thirteen

Sophie pressed her ear against the closet door, listening to the footsteps approaching. A man's heavy tread. Was it the same guy as before, or someone new? Only one person, she thought, so the first man hadn't gone for help.

The steps headed straight for the bedroom. She held her breath, afraid to even breathe. The bed creaked, then two thunks—had he removed his shoes and dropped them on the floor? The mattress creaked again, and someone sighed. Was he settling in for a nap?

She waited for several minutes, straining to hear, but all was silent. Finally, she wrapped her hand around the doorknob and turned it ever so slowly, then eased it open, easy…easy…

She pressed one eye to the narrow opening and stared out at a bulky man in desert camo, stretched out on his back on the bed, hands folded on his chest like a corpse. Maybe he'd been the one who came into the room before, only a call had forced him to delay his nap. Another call could wake him at any time—especially a call that Prentice was returning to the ranch.

The man on the bed snored, making her jump. She shut the door and leaned her forehead against the smooth wood. *Think!* she silently commanded herself. She had to get out of here. Once Prentice returned, she'd be trapped. She'd probably only been able to get in because the guards had relaxed a little with their boss gone. When he returned, they'd be on their best—and sharpest—behavior.

The snoring continued, heavy and even. The guy was really out of it. This had to be her best chance to get by him.

She eased the door open once more, then slipped out of the closet. The sleeping man's chest rose and fell evenly, his snores like the rumble of a motorbike. On tiptoe, Sophie crossed the room. He'd shut the door, so she had to stop and deal with that. She turned the doorknob and tugged, expecting it to open easily, as all the other doors had. But this one stuck. She tugged again and it opened suddenly, sending her lurching back. Worse, the hinges let out a tortured squeal. Sophie cringed, and started into the hall.

"You there! Stop!" The voice, deep and commanding, had the force of a bullet hitting her back, but she hesitated only a moment before taking off down the hall. No sense worrying about being quiet now; she ran as hard as she could, feet pounding along the hall and down the stairs. Behind her, the guard shouted and raced after her.

She crossed the kitchen, slipping a little on the tile, then regained her balance and hurtled through the mudroom, hitting the back door hard, fumbling for the knob. Behind her a second guard had taken up the pursuit. "Stop, or I'll shoot!"

She stumbled down the steps and darted across the prairie, aiming for the fences and the road in the distance. She'd only gone a few dozen yards when the first bullets whistled past her. She'd read before that it was hard to hit a moving target, but that didn't mean it was impossible, was it?

Her side ached, and every breath was torture, her lungs burning. Why hadn't she kept up her New Year's resolution to go to the gym more? Maybe the bullets wouldn't have to kill her; she'd collapse on the prairie from exhaustion. She glanced over her shoulder and let out a wail when she saw the Jeep barreling toward her. Oh, God, they were going to catch her. What would they do to her?

She tried to run faster, but she stumbled and sprawled forward, the breath knocked from her. She lay facedown in the rocks and bunch grass, trying to breathe, waiting for the shot she was sure would end her life. Tears squeezed from beneath her closed eyes. So much for being brave; her foolishness had cost her everything.

The Jeep stopped somewhere behind her and footsteps approached. "Get up," a man's voice commanded.

She didn't move. Maybe they'd think she was already dead and go away. Or did that only work with bears?

Rough hands grabbed her arms and hauled her to her feet. "Who are you?" the guard—the one who'd been napping on the bed—demanded. Up close, he looked much younger, only in his early twenties, she thought, with a sunburned, unlined face and blond stubble on choirboy rosy cheeks.

She kept her mouth shut. If she didn't say anything, they couldn't use the information against her.

"What are you doing here?" The other guard, older and beefier, like a linebacker, had climbed out of the Jeep and walked toward her.

She looked away and tried to assume a bored expression. She doubted she was fooling anybody, especially since her knees were visibly shaking.

"Were you trying to steal something?" the older guard asked. "Did you take anything?"

"Maybe we should search her." The younger guard leered at her.

If he tried, she'd kick him where it hurt. Wasn't that what they taught in all those female self-defense classes at the Y?

Something behind them distracted them. She followed their gaze and saw the dust plume that indicated an approaching vehicle. "Mr. Prentice is back," the older guard said.

"Come on." The first guard dragged her toward the Jeep. "Let's go talk to him."

"If you let me go, I won't tell him you were napping on the job," she said.

The younger guard gave her a sour look but didn't stop walking. "I don't know what you're talking about," he said.

The older guard shot them a curious look, but he didn't slow down, either. So she'd have to throw herself on Prentice's mercy. He'd been perfectly civil to her when he invited her to his home, but chances were he wouldn't view her return visit so favorably.

The Jeep and Prentice's SUV met in front of the house. The guards hauled her out and brought her to stand in front of Prentice and two men in dark suits. His lawyers, she guessed. All three men regarded her sourly. "Ms. Montgomery," Prentice said. "What are you doing here?"

"I came to see you," she said. "But you weren't at home."

"How did you get past the guards?"

She shrugged. "Maybe they were occupied elsewhere. I didn't see any reason not to come up to the house."

"Oh, you didn't?" Prentice looked her up and down, with the attitude of a man who had ordered a new suit and found it not to his liking. "You have no business on my property. I could have you jailed for trespassing."

"I came to see you. That's not the same as trespassing."

"She was in the house," the younger guard said. "In the upstairs bedroom."

Prentice's scowl deepened.

"I was waiting for you to come home," Sophie said. "You have a very nice house, so I thought I'd look around. I didn't hurt anything. I didn't take anything." Except pictures.

"We should search her, to be sure," the older guard said.

"We should call the police and have her arrested," one of the lawyers said.

"It seems someone has already summoned them." The others followed Prentice's gaze to the vehicles speeding down the drive toward them. Sophie sagged with relief as she recognized the black-and-white FJ Cruisers used by The Ranger Brigade.

The SUVs stopped and Rand and Graham stepped out. They both wore dark sunglasses, so she couldn't read their expressions, but the hard set of their mouths told her they weren't pleased to be here. "We had a report of a trespasser," Rand said.

"Who made the report?" Prentice asked. He showed no sign of recognizing Rand from his previous visit, when he'd posed as Sophie's boyfriend. Maybe the uniform, or Rand's commanding attitude, distracted him. "I didn't call anyone."

"Then someone who works for you must have called us." He moved toward her, long strides covering ground quickly.

"We know how much you value your privacy," Graham said.

Rand wrapped his hand around her upper arm. The touch wasn't gentle, but it reassured her, nonetheless. He might be angry with her, but she trusted him to keep her safe. "We'll take her now," he said. "Do you want to press charges?"

Prentice regarded her coldly for a long moment, as if weighing his options. "No charges," he said. "But I want to know what she is doing here."

"I told you. I wanted to talk to you—about my sister."

"I've already told you everything I know about your sister," Prentice said.

"I was hoping you might have remembered something else. Something that would help us find her."

"Maybe your sister doesn't want to be found," he said. "Maybe she's started a new life and is happy with her new circumstances."

"She knows I only want her to be happy," Sophie said. "Why would she hide that from me?"

"Sometimes the best way to start over is to cut all ties with the past," Prentice said.

"Not with the only family you have," Sophie said. "Lauren wouldn't do that."

"My advice to you is to go back to Wisconsin and get on with your life," he said. "I'm sure Lauren is fine."

"Do you know something we don't?" Rand asked.

"I'm merely being logical. You haven't found a body or anything to indicate that Lauren Starling is dead. She was at a difficult place in her life. Why not make a fresh start, perhaps with a new name, in a new place? It happens more than most people think. There's nothing criminal in it."

"Lauren wouldn't turn her back on me," Sophie said. "I know she wouldn't."

Prentice turned to the Rangers. "Take her away," he said. "Then all of you, get off my property."

She and Rand followed Graham out of the house. "I'll see you at headquarters," Graham said, and climbed into his vehicle.

Rand dragged her toward his FJ Cruiser, where Lotte greeted them with a sharp bark. She hardly noticed the dog, she was so focused on the man beside her. Gone was the gentleness he'd shown her earlier. He held his body rigid, his jaw clenched, as he started the vehicle and pulled away, tires squealing and gravel pinging against the undercarriage. "I'm sorry I upset you," she said when they'd cleared the ranch gates.

"Upset me?" He slammed on the brakes and skidded to the side of the road, so violently she clutched the dashboard to keep from being thrown forward. "Of all the stupid, ill-conceived, foolhardy stunts—you could have been killed." His voice shook with some emotion she couldn't name—anger, frustration...fear?

"But I wasn't killed." She struggled to keep her own voice even. "You showed up at just the right time. And I'm very grateful for that." She'd never been so glad to see anyone in her life.

"Didn't what happened yesterday at your hotel

teach you anything about the kind of people we're dealing with here?" he asked. "I thought you were smart enough to be afraid."

"Of course I'm scared," she said. "But I'm more afraid of what will happen to Lauren if we don't find her soon. I had to do something."

"It's my job to find your sister." The anger had left his voice, and his expression grew gentle again.

"I know you're doing what you can, but it's not enough." She swallowed against the sudden threat of tears. "Maybe what I did wasn't smart, but I got the proof you need to get a warrant to search Prentice's house."

"You obtained the proof illegally. We can't use it in court."

"But you can use it to get your warrant."

"What proof do you have?" he asked a little more calmly.

"I have pictures." She held up her phone and he leaned over to peer at the image.

"What am I looking at?" he asked.

"It's a woman's purse, with a business card inside. Lauren's card. It proves she was in the house—I know it."

RAND DIDN'T KNOW whether to kiss Sophie or shake her. She really thought she'd done the best thing, going into Prentice's house when he wasn't home, but she could have jeopardized their whole case, not to mention her life. He shook his head and put the vehicle in gear again. "We'll talk about it more at headquarters." Maybe the captain could explain it to her better. He was obviously too emotionally involved to view anything she did impartially.

"Are you really arresting me for trespassing?" she asked when he turned into the lot in front of the Ranger headquarters.

"I ought to." He shut off the engine but made no move to get out of the vehicle. "What you did was incredibly foolish and dangerous." And he broke into a cold sweat, just thinking about it.

"Playing it safe isn't finding Lauren."

She sounded stubborn now. He turned to her. "I don't think you realize that what you did could jeopardize the whole investigation."

"Or it could solve all your problems."

"Your sister's disappearance isn't the only crime we're trying to solve here. If it is a crime."

She stiffened. "What do you mean?"

"What if Lauren is with Prentice—but she's with him voluntarily? What if it's like he said— she's trying to start over and cut ties to the past?"

"She wouldn't do that." Was that doubt in her voice?

"Why not?" he asked. "The man's a billionaire. He's always being photographed with beautiful women, so he must have some charms. His last girlfriend was a Venezuelan fashion model. Maybe Lauren really likes him."

"She wouldn't disappear without telling me."

"Didn't you say she'd dropped out of sight for a while once before?"

"That was before her diagnosis. Now she's being careful, taking her medication…"

"People relapse. I don't know a lot about bipolar, but I've been doing a little reading. Apparently, sometimes people enjoy the manic periods so much they're reluctant to let them go. They go off their medication, believing they can handle themselves this time, but then they fall back into the old cycles. Maybe that's what happened to your sister."

Tears sparkled in her eyes, and he felt like a jerk for causing her such pain. But better that she face facts now than be doubly hurt if he turned out to be right later. "I've read those things, too," she said. "But even when she was sickest, Lauren never stayed out of touch with me this long. And she loved her job."

"She doesn't need a job if Prentice is supporting her."

She looked away, cheeks flushed, mouth set in a stubborn line. "So you have this neat little theory of what happened to her. Does that mean you're going to stop looking?"

"No. We're going to keep looking. But you have to stay out of the way and let us do our jobs." He softened his tone. "I don't want you to get hurt."

She nodded. "I know. And…that means a lot to me." She opened the car door. "Let's go in and see what everyone else has to say."

He released Lotte from the back and the three of them walked up to Ranger headquarters. Sophie didn't shy away from the dog as much now, though she still avoided looking at or touching her. Baby steps, he reminded himself. At least she could be in the same room with the dog now without freaking out.

Most of the other Rangers were gathered around the conference table when they arrived. Carmen, who stood at the head of the table, looked up when they arrived. "The CSI report on the fish shop just came in," she said. She looked at Sophie. "Maybe you should go into another room."

"I don't care about the fish shop," she said. "Besides, I don't have anyone to tell."

"She's okay." Rand steered her to a chair along the back wall. "What's in the report?"

"Drugs," Carmen said. "Lots and lots of drugs. Milbanks had received a shipment of fish from the Gulf of Mexico that morning. One of the investigators cut open a big amberjack and it was full of balloons of heroin. Another contained a bag of cocaine."

"So the local cops were right that the fish shop was just a front for drug smuggling?" Michael asked.

Carmen nodded. "It was a pretty slick operation, from what we can determine. Milbanks owned a fleet of fishing boats. They'd catch the fish, then load them up with drugs, put them on ice and fly them up here. He'd remove the drugs, load them on trucks to be distributed elsewhere, then sell the fish to local restaurants and individuals. He made money on both ventures and looked like a legitimate businessman."

"He could be the guy we've been looking for," Graham said. "The kingpin in charge of the increased activity in the region."

"He had the money and the contacts," Carmen said.

"That doesn't mean Richard Prentice wasn't involved," Rand said. "The picture of him and Milbanks together proves they knew each other."

"Maybe they were working together, or maybe the picture relates to something else," Graham said. "We don't know."

"Whoever killed him left behind all those drugs?" Simon asked.

"Maybe they didn't know about the drugs," Carmen said. "Or they didn't care."

"Did the investigators find anything in the shop to connect Milbanks and Prentice?" Rand asked.

"Nothing," Carmen said. "And nothing to tie Milbanks to Lauren Starling, either. We do think we know where the picture of Milbanks and Prentice together was taken, though."

"Where?" Rand asked.

"Behind the shop," Simon said. "The parking lot has a security camera trained near the door. The video analyst who studied the photograph recognized a pattern in the brick behind the men. She thinks the photograph is probably an enlarged frame from video taken by that camera."

"Milbanks could have gotten the picture from his own security system," Michael said. "Maybe that's what he was giving to Lauren the day he met her at the motel."

"But why give her something like that?" Simon asked.

"There's some indication that Milbanks may have been preparing to leave the country," Carmen said. "The investigators found airline tickets to the Cayman Islands in his desk drawer. He was supposed to fly out yesterday. We believe he may have planned to process this last shipment of drugs and fish, then get out of town before authorities caught up with him again. He probably has money stashed in accounts in the Caymans."

"But someone murdered him before he could leave," Rand said.

"Maybe he was killed because of the photograph," Sophie suggested. They all swiveled to look at her. "Maybe Prentice found out he'd given the photograph to Lauren."

"How would he find out?" Rand asked. "The photograph was still in her car."

"Maybe she told him," Sophie said.

"Right now Lauren Starling is the only one who can answer these questions," Graham said. "We have to find her."

"The calls we've been making checking on Lauren's background did turn up one interesting fact," Carmen said. She consulted her notes. "She had a one-million-dollar life insurance policy through her employer. The beneficiary is her ex-husband, Phillip Starling."

Michael whistled. "So he had at least one reason to want Lauren out of the picture. Especially if he was having money problems."

"Why wouldn't she have changed the beneficiary on the policy when they divorced?" Rand asked Sophie.

"Lauren wasn't always good about following up on that kind of detail," she said. "And money wasn't really that big a deal to her. She might have even wanted Phil to have the money—part of her still cared about him."

"So Phil is still on our list of suspects," Rand said.

A phone rang. Graham shifted in his chair to pull out his cell. "Hello?"

He listened for a few moments, then ended the call. "Marco is on his way with the warrant to search Richard Prentice's home," he said.

"Then my photographs helped," Sophie said.

"Your photographs, along with the photo of Prentice and Milbanks together, were enough to persuade the judge that we had grounds to investigate further," Graham said.

"I want to go with you," she said.

"No." Rand spoke before anyone else could answer. "You have to stay here." He didn't want her anywhere near Prentice again.

She frowned but had sense enough not to argue. "Then let me go back to my hotel room."

"I can't let you do that, either. It's not safe."

She looked around the utilitarian room. "What am I supposed to do while you're away?"

"You can go back to my place." Could he trust her to stay put this time?

"I've got an idea," Graham said. "Some place she'll be safe and out of trouble, but more comfortable." He took out his phone and punched in a number. "Emma? How would you like some company this afternoon?"

Chapter Fourteen

Sophie rode with Rand to Graham and Emma's house. Awkward silence still stretched between them. His anger annoyed her, though she told herself it was merely a sign of how much he cared. But it rankled that he wouldn't give her credit for helping his investigation. As if the work the cops did was the only kind that mattered.

He pulled up to the house and shifted into Park. "I'll call and let you know what we find out," he said, not looking at her.

She nodded and opened the door. But she couldn't leave with this coldness between them. "Be careful," she said softly. "I've already lost one person who's important to me. I don't want to lose another."

She didn't wait for his reaction, but slid from the car and hurried up the walk to the house, where Emma welcomed her. "Come on in," she said, ushering her into the living room.

"Hey." Abby looked up from the sofa, where

she was petting a large gray tabby. "We're glad you could come."

"Thanks for having me," Sophie said. "I really didn't want to hang around Ranger headquarters alone." Or at Rand's house. There were too many unanswered questions between them for her to feel comfortable there.

"It's our pleasure," Emma said.

"We're hoping you can fill us in on everything that's going on," Abby said.

Sophie settled onto the sofa opposite Abby. "There's not much to tell. Apparently, Alan Milbanks was smuggling drugs in his fish, and they think he was getting ready to leave the country when he was killed. I found a closet full of women's clothing in an upstairs bedroom at Richard Prentice's ranch. The clothes were Lauren's size, and they smelled of her perfume."

"I can't believe you went out there on your own," Abby said. "Weren't you scared?"

"Yes." She still got shaky, thinking about it. "But my worry about Lauren was stronger than my fear."

"You're lucky the Rangers got to you before Prentice did," Emma said.

"Do you really think he's dangerous?" Sophie asked. The billionaire was stern and grumpy and imperious, but he seemed too urbane to be violent.

"Remember what I told you—the last time I was at his ranch someone drugged me and knocked me out," Emma said. "I was thrown down a mine shaft and left to die."

"It's hard to picture Richard Prentice doing something so violent," Sophie said. The man was so cold and businesslike.

"We don't have any proof, but I think it was one of his guards," Emma said. "The mine was located not far from his land, in the Curecanti wilderness area. Graham rescued me, though he was injured in the process."

"Several people have died who had connections to Prentice," Abby said.

"Then why is he still free?" Sophie asked. It didn't make sense.

"Because he's very rich and very smart," Emma said. "No one's been able to come up with strong proof to tie him to the crimes that are happening all around him."

"What kind of crimes?" Sophie asked.

"All the things the Rangers were formed to investigate and prevent," Abby said. "Last month they broke up a big illegal marijuana-growing and human-trafficking operation within the park. The man who was overseeing that had ties to a Mexican drug cartel, but the Rangers believe he wasn't operating independently, that he had someone local who was financing the operation.

The man—Raul Meredes—was shot by a sniper before he could talk to authorities."

"A friend of mine, a pilot who flew for Prentice, was murdered while smuggling a stolen Hellfire missile," Emma said. "He landed in Black Canyon of the Gunnison National Park and was shot by the woman who had hired him for the job—the daughter of the Venezuelan ambassador to the United States."

"Who was also Richard Prentice's girlfriend," Abby said. "She was caught on Prentice's ranch with the missile."

"What did she want with a Hellfire missile?" Sophie asked.

"We're not sure." Emma took up the story again. "Some people believe she planned to pass it along to terrorists in her homeland. In that case, Prentice may have financed the purchase. Or she might have gotten it for Prentice himself, to arm the unmanned drone he's rumored to have purchased."

"That's the problem," Abby said. "All of this is merely rumors and theory. Prentice may not have known anything about the missile. Valentina—the ambassador's daughter—may have just been taking advantage of her connection to him."

"The human-trafficking operation was happening all around him," Emma said. "But no one has proof he knew anything about it. Maybe he's telling the truth and he really is innocent."

"That doesn't explain what women's clothing in Lauren's size, smelling of Lauren's perfume, is doing in a closet in his home," Sophie said. "And he admits he knows her."

"He can't really deny that," Emma said. "They attended the same charity ball in Denver not that long ago. It was in the paper."

"Did they find any luggage in your sister's car when she disappeared?" Abby asked.

Sophie shook her head. "None. Her laptop and phone are missing, too."

"Then maybe she's somewhere hiding?" Abby said, speculating. "Or she's with Prentice voluntarily?"

"That's what Rand suggested, too," Sophie said. "But I don't believe it. She wouldn't hide from me. She has no reason to."

"Families are funny." Abby hugged a pillow to her chest. "Sometimes the people we love the most are the ones we need to get away from the most."

"What do you mean?" Sophie asked.

"I was injured in the war," Abby said. "That's where I got this." She tucked her hair behind one ear and traced the scar along her cheek. "My parents were so worried and upset. They tried hard to protect me and encourage me at the same time, but all their hovering was too much. I felt like I was smothering. That's one reason I struck out on my own and came here. It wasn't that I didn't love them, just that I needed to figure out things on my own. I needed to live the life I wanted, not the one they wanted for me."

"So you're saying that Lauren might have felt smothered by me?" The words pained her to say them.

"She had a lot to deal with," Abby said. "Her diagnosis, divorce, problems at work. I can see how that would be overwhelming."

"And I've always been the big sister, looking after her." Sophie nodded. "I guess in her place, I might have found that a little smothering, too. But all she had to do was tell me to back off. I would have respected that. She didn't have to cut ties altogether. With everyone."

"Maybe the Rangers will find something at Prentice's ranch today," Emma said. "Maybe they'll even find her and she can tell us herself what's going on."

GRAHAM, MICHAEL, RAND and Lotte pulled up to the gates at the Prentice Ranch a little after three in the afternoon, where Graham presented their search warrant to the guard who walked out to greet them. "Wait here and I'll consult with Mr. Prentice," the guard said, and started to turn away.

"No, we won't wait." Graham shifted the FJ Cruiser into gear. "We'll go on up to the house. Now." He gunned the engine, forcing the guard to jump out of the way or be run over.

"He must have called ahead," Rand said as they neared the house. Prentice, flanked by the two lawyers, waited for them in front of the massive oak door.

"I strongly object to this violation of my client's privacy." The younger lawyer began speaking before the Rangers were even out of the car.

"Object all you like. We have a legal warrant." Graham held the papers out to Prentice.

The billionaire put his hands behind his back, his face impassive.

Graham opened his hand and let the papers flutter to the ground at Prentice's feet. "Come on." He addressed the others. "We'll start upstairs."

Lotte led the way, trotting up the stairs ahead of them. She stopped and waited on the landing at the top. Rand pulled a handkerchief from his pocket, one he'd scented with the Mitsouko perfume he'd ordered from a department store in Denver two days earlier. *"Sic,"* he commanded, and Lotte hesitated only a moment before heading down the hall.

Rand trotted to keep up with the dog, the others following. Lotte stopped and whined at a closed door. Rand slipped on a pair of gloves, then carefully opened the door. The dog rushed in and stopped again beside an ornate carved bed.

"Does she think Lauren Starling's been in that bed?" Michael asked from behind him.

"Someone wearing this perfume, in any case." He glanced under the bed. Nothing there but dust. "Let's try the closet."

Michael opened the closet door and the three men and the dog crowded around to look in. Lotte whined excitedly, her signal for a find. But the closet was empty. Not so much as a coat hanger disturbed the space.

"Is this the closet Sophie said was full of women's clothes and shoes?" Graham asked.

"According to the diagram she drew for us, yes." Rand frowned. Even he recognized the scent of the Mitsouko perfume in here, but the space looked as if it had been empty for a while. He ran a finger along the edge of the shelf. It came away dirty—the kind of dust that collected when a space sat unused for a long time.

"Come on, let's see what else is up here." Graham led the way out of the room.

Looking confused, Lotte followed. She kept looking back over the shoulder at Rand, her expression worried. When she found what they were looking for, everyone was supposed to be happy. They weren't supposed to ask her to keep looking. But she obediently sniffed every corner of every room they entered and found nothing.

Downstairs proved just as empty, of anything but Prentice's furniture and books and personal belongings. The longer they searched, the more visibly frustrated Graham grew. Downstairs, Prentice and his duo of dark-suited attorneys followed them from room to room, the billionaire's expression growing more and more smug.

When they had searched every room, even looking into the washer and dryer and every cabinet and closet, Graham snapped off his gloves and stuffed them into his pocket. "We're done here," he said. "Thank you for your cooperation."

"You will be hearing from us," the older attorney said.

Back in the SUV, Graham remained impassive until they were on the road headed back to headquarters. He slammed one hand against the dash, making them jump. "How is it he's always one step ahead of us?" he asked.

"Maybe there's another possibility we need to consider here," Michael said.

"What's that?" Rand asked.

Michael looked away "Maybe Sophie is making all this up."

Rand stiffened. "Lotte alerted on that closet. Even I could smell the perfume in there."

"Maybe because Sophie put it in there. We're only taking her word for it that Lauren even wears that perfume."

"What about the photographs she showed us?" Rand asked. "Those weren't fake."

"They were photographs taken in a closet of some women's clothes and shoes," Michael said. "That could have been any closet. That could have been any purse with a business card in it. There's nothing to show where the pictures were taken. If we tried to introduce them in court, a good lawyer would say the same thing."

Rand shook his head, disoriented. "Why would she do that? Why go to so much trouble to lie to us?"

"Because she wants attention?" Michael shrugged. "Maybe she's as unbalanced as her sister."

Rand's stomach heaved. "No."

"I'm not saying that's what happened," Michael said. "But until we find more evidence to support her claims, we have to consider the possibility."

"No," Rand said again. "I've spent a lot of time with her these last couple of days. She's worried about her sister, sure, but nothing about her struck me as off or unstable."

"Maybe you're letting your feelings for her get in the way of your judgment."

Rand realized he'd curled both hands into fists. He'd never felt so much like punching his friend. He turned to Graham. "What do you think, Captain?"

"Sophie has spent the last three hours with Emma and Abby," he said. "I think they're both good judges of character. Let's ask them what they think."

BY THE TIME RAND, Graham and Michael joined them at the captain's house, the three women were like old friends. They'd spent the afternoon discussing the wedding plans for Emma and Graham, and Michael and Abby. From there the conversation had moved on to books they'd read, music they enjoyed and jobs they'd held. They were sharing "worst boss ever" stories when the men showed up. Quickly, their attention shifted to the investigation.

"What did you find?" Emma asked, before Graham had even settled onto the sofa beside her.

"Nothing." Graham rubbed the back of his neck with one hand. "We didn't find anything at all incriminating in that house."

"But the closet…" Sophie began.

"The closet was empty," Rand said. His eyes met hers, his expression hard and cold.

"Then he must have cleaned it out as soon as I left," she said. "The guard would have told him I was in that bedroom. He'd have known what I saw, and that I'd tell you."

"Or maybe you were…mistaken," Michael said.

"There was no mistake in what I saw," she said. "And what about the pictures I took?"

He shrugged. "Prentice's attorney would say those pictures could have been taken anywhere. There was nothing to prove they were taken in Prentice's house."

Feeling sick, Sophie turned to Rand. "You believe me, don't you?"

"I want to believe you."

She turned away, not wanting him to see her hurt.

"You all have spent too much time around criminals." Emma's voice cut through the silence. "Sophie isn't lying, any more than I was lying about seeing women's cosmetics in Prentice's bathroom."

"Do you really think Sophie came all this way to stage some elaborate hoax?" Abby asked. She sounded indignant.

"No," Rand said. "I think we're all frustrated at our lack of progress." He glared at Michael.

Michael looked away. "I was just playing devil's advocate," he said. "It's important to look at an investigation from all angles."

"So, what did you find at the house?" Emma asked. "What did Prentice say?"

Graham began describing their visit to the house. Sophie turned away. She wasn't interested in any of this.

"I'm sorry." Rand gripped her shoulder and turned her to face him. "Of course I believe you."

"I wasn't lying," she said. "I didn't stage the photos or make anything up."

"I know that," he said. "Why would you? You want your sister safe. I want that, too."

He opened his arms and she went to him, letting him hold her, her head resting against his chest. She felt bone-weary and discouraged, too exhausted almost to stand. "This must be what it's like for Lauren all the time," she said.

"What do you mean?"

"Having people judge you, second-guess you, question your motives. Her illness has led her to do some ill-advised things in the past, but that doesn't mean everything she does is irrational or because of her illness. Most of the time she's as rational and ordinary as the rest of us. But a lot of people can't see her that way, because of things that happened when she wasn't well. It must make everything so much harder. It's why she wanted so much to prove herself to her bosses. She wanted to show them that she was still an asset to the station, that she was still a good reporter."

"We have the testimony of the hotel clerk that she met Alan Milbanks there, and we found the photograph in her car of Milbanks with Prentice," Rand said. "Milbanks was involved in drug smuggling and distribution. Maybe Lauren uncovered that and confronted him. That made him angry and he—or someone he hired—decided to silence her."

Sophie shuddered at his words. Not that she hadn't made herself face that her sister might not be alive after all this time, but hearing someone else say as much was hard to bear. "If Milbanks was her target, what did she gain by confronting him at the hotel?" she asked. "Why not just go to the police with whatever evidence she had? Her story would be his arrest and conviction. She had nothing to gain by taunting him."

"Then what was she doing, meeting with him?"

"What if Milbanks promised to cooperate with her by revealing someone higher up the food chain?" Sophie asked. "He gave her the photograph as proof, but then that person—Richard Prentice?—found out."

"That would explain both Lauren's disappearance and Milbanks's murder," Rand said. "Except, so far at least, we don't have any evidence that Prentice is linked to either of those crimes."

"What will you do now?" she asked.

"We'll keep digging. Maybe focus on Milbanks, look at his financial records, phone records, talk to people who knew him. We'll try to get as complete a picture as possible of how he operated. That may help us figure out how he knew Lauren, and if Prentice is involved at all."

Paperwork. She had no doubt this kind of research was important, but they needed action to rescue her sister. "Meanwhile, Lauren is still out there, missing."

He caressed her shoulder. "I know it's hard. I wish I could do more. We'll keep searching for her, I promise."

"I know she wouldn't go this long without contacting me. And now I'm more sure than ever that Richard Prentice is the 'Mr. Wonderful' she mentioned in her letter. But what has he done with her?"

"I don't know. But I'm ready to listen to any ideas you have."

"Are you, really?" She studied the eyes she couldn't help thinking of as kind, the strong slant of his nose, the firm jut of his chin. He wasn't movie-star handsome, but he had strength and character, and she trusted him not to lie to her. "You don't think I'm being hysterical, or mentally unbalanced, or obsessed?" she asked. "You don't think I'm making things up?"

"No. I believe you care for your sister very much, and you're doing everything you can to see that she's safe."

She glanced toward the others, who had moved to the kitchen and were making sandwiches. "Your coworkers don't feel the same. They think I'm making all this up. Maybe they don't even believe I'm Lauren's sister."

He winced. "Cops are trained to be suspicious. It's a useful trait for an investigator, and sometimes it keeps us alive."

"I believe Lauren is still alive. And after what I saw today, I think she's with Richard Prentice."

"We searched everywhere in that house and we didn't find so much as a hair."

"He's hiding her, then. He moved her and all her things when he knew you all were coming."

"We didn't call ahead and warn him," he said.

"You said yourself, he has contacts everywhere. Someone from the judge's office could have called him. Or he might have figured out what I'd seen and moved her in case I came back."

"Yes, that could have happened. But where would he hide her?"

"Some place close. Probably still on the ranch. Did you search any outbuildings?"

"Our warrant was only for the main house and garage. The property has some other structures on it, everything from housing for his guards to log bunkhouses dating from the late eighteen hundreds."

"Lauren could be in any one of those. How can you get back there to look?"

"I don't think he'd use one of those other buildings and risk her being seen. He knows we fly surveillance over the property occasionally."

"He could put her in a vehicle and drive her to wherever she was going," Sophie said.

"Or he could use a tunnel."

She frowned. "A tunnel?"

"We've heard rumors that he has a tunnel connecting the house to an old mine near the house," Rand said. "We thought he might be using the mine to hide contraband, but we never got a look inside." He took her arm. "Let's run this by the others and see what they think."

When they walked into the kitchen, Emma looked up from spreading mustard on a slice of bread. "Do you two want something to eat?" she asked. "I've got ham and turkey, and a couple of different kinds of cheese."

"Not right now, thanks." He turned to Graham. "Captain, I have an idea where Prentice might be hiding Lauren."

Graham swallowed a bite of sandwich. "What's your idea?"

"Maybe he has her in that mine—the one where we thought he'd stashed the missile? Supposedly there's a tunnel that connects the mine to the house. It would be easy to move a person there from the house without being seen."

"I looked for any kind of secret passage or door when we were in the house today," Michael said. "I didn't find anything."

"It could be a very sophisticated mechanism, one we wouldn't be able to find without special equipment we didn't have with us today," Rand said.

"Even if you're right, I don't know what we can do about it," Graham said. "By this time Prentice is raising so much hell in the press and with every politician he has in his pocket that a judge will never give us another search warrant."

"Then we go in without a warrant. We sneak in at night."

"That's illegal," Graham said. "And it's dangerous. If he is hiding someone—or something—in that mine, he'll have guards watching."

"We'll avoid the guards," Rand said. "Or I could go in alone. No sense risking anyone else."

"I'd go with you," Sophie said.

"Do that and I really will arrest you for trespassing," Graham said.

"Do you think I care about that when my sister could be in danger?"

"Let me go, Captain," Rand said. "If I get caught, you can suspend me and deny any knowledge."

"I wouldn't do that. In this organization, we've always got each other's backs." He pressed his lips together, silent for a moment. Sophie waited, scarcely breathing, the muscles in Rand's arm tense beneath her hand.

"Take Marco with you," Graham said. "You'll have to hike in from federal land."

Rand nodded. "We'll go tonight, about ten. There's no moon, but the weather is supposed to be clear. I'll get with Marco now to start planning."

He turned to Sophie. "You'll be all right here, won't you?"

"Take me back to your place," she said. "Emma has to cover a council meeting tonight for her paper and Graham will be working." She wouldn't be comfortable staying by herself with the gruff captain.

"All right." He patted her hand. "Wish me luck."

"Good luck. And…thank you."

He pulled her close. "I'll do my best to find her."

She nodded, unable to speak. As much as she wanted Lauren safe, what if she lost Rand in the process?

Chapter Fifteen

Rand and Marco set out in the dark, with backpacks and night-vision goggles. They'd spent the early evening studying the layout of Prentice's ranch, choosing the best approach to the old mine. They'd decided to approach from the rear, over rugged country, reasoning that this section of the ranch would be less heavily patrolled. The guards would expect a threat to come from the front of the ranch, from the road.

The going was tough, scrabbling up loose talus slopes, climbing down into cactus-choked gorges. The two didn't say much, communicating mostly in grunts and hand gestures, focused on the task at hand. They saw the lights from the house long before they could make out the structure itself, the floodlights sending up a pink glow like the light pollution from a small city, blotting out the stars.

When the building itself was in view, Marco thrust out a hand, signaling to stop. He pointed in the distance, and Rand made out the pinpoints of two headlights. The lights drew closer and closer, the vehicle in no hurry, crawling over the rough terrain. The two men flattened themselves, faces pressed to the ground. Rand could hear the rumble of the Jeep's engine now, and the growl of tires on gravel. The beams of light passed over their heads, and then were gone. Rand crawled closer to Marco. "Did you get a look at them?" he asked.

"Two of Prentice's guards," Marco said. "Regular patrol. They shouldn't be back this way for an hour, at least."

Marco led the way toward the old mine. Iron bars set too close together for anything larger than a pack rat to pass through blocked the entrance, a common safety precaution in a country littered with abandoned shafts. Marco motioned to move around to the side. Two hundred yards farther on they found a second entrance, a dark hole with cool air coming from it. They peered inside and saw a single guard, leaning against the wall, dozing.

Rand nudged Marco. *Bingo.* Why set a guard over an abandoned mine unless there was something inside worth guarding?

Marco motioned that he would go first and Rand should cover. Both men drew their duty weapons. Marco crept along the passage, keeping close to the wall. When he reached the dozing guard, he clamped one hand over his mouth and twisted his arm back and up, forcing him to his knees.

Rand hurried forward and together they tied up and gagged the guard. Rand shouldered the AR-15 the man had carried, and Marco pocketed his pistol. "We don't have long now," Marco said. "They probably have to check in at regular intervals."

They moved on down the passage, which was tall enough for them to walk upright, one behind the other. Rand's heart raced and cold sweat beaded on his forehead. He'd never particularly liked enclosed spaces. He forced himself to take deep, even breaths of the cool, dusty air. "What's that smell?" he asked, wrinkling his nose at the ammonia-tinged odor.

"Bats," Marco said. "They like caves and old mine shafts."

"I wish we had Lotte with us. She'd probably take us right to Lauren if she's here."

"It's harder to be stealthy with a dog," Marco said.

"Lotte can be stealthy, but I thought it would be better to leave her with Sophie."

"I thought she was afraid of dogs."

"She is, but Lotte will protect her."

Sophie had protested when he insisted on leaving the dog, but the memory of the slashed underwear and the menacing message in her hotel room made him adamant. "She won't hurt you," he'd reassured her. "But she will hurt anyone who comes after you."

"There's a light up ahead," Marco said softly.

Rand spotted the faint glow from the side passage. They moved faster toward it, but stopped abruptly when they spotted a second guard. This one was awake, pacing back and forth. Marco's eyes met Rand's. *Rush him*, he mouthed, and Rand nodded.

Guns drawn, the two rushed the guard, and were on him before he could ready his weapon to fire. "What are you guarding, pal?" Rand asked as he bound the man's wrists with plastic zip ties.

"Why should I tell you?"

"Suit yourself." Marco stuffed a gag in the man's mouth and slapped on a strip of duct tape. "Let's go." He jerked his head toward the passage the guard had been watching over.

The room was dimly lit with two lanterns hung from nails on opposite walls, and set up like a bedroom, complete with a queen-sized bed, a dresser and a fuzzy pink rug beneath their feet. Someone stirred beneath the heap of quilts on the bed, then sat up, staring at them.

"Lauren Starling," Marco said, and she began to scream.

SOPHIE SAT RIGID on the sofa in Rand's duplex, hands clenched tightly in her lap, her breathing shallow. Every few seconds she glanced at the dog who lay on her pad in the corner, mouth open to reveal gleaming white teeth, golden eyes fixed on Sophie.

She'd argued with Rand when he insisted on leaving the dog with her, but he'd been stubborn. "She'll protect you," he'd said.

"I'm afraid of her." Something he would never understand.

"Then now is a good time for you to get to know her, to work on getting over your fear." He squeezed her arm. "I've seen how strong you are. How brave you are. If you can risk Prentice's guards, you can risk spending a few hours with Lotte."

"How is she going to protect me?"

"She'll hear someone coming before you will. And she's trained to defend me with her life. She'll do the same for you."

"Leave me a gun. I can protect myself."

His expression grew skeptical. "How much shooting have you done?

"None."

"Then Lotte will be better protection," he'd concluded.

She looked at the dog again, trying to see

her objectively as a beautiful animal. Her fur gleamed in the lamplight, gold with black tips, thick and looking as soft as a Persian rug. Dark hair ringed her eyes, making her appear to be wearing eyeliner, and her lashes were as long and lush as any starlet's. The idea almost made Sophie giggle. She must have made some sound, because Lotte pricked up her ears and cocked her head in a quizzical gesture.

"I'm sure you think I'm crazy," Sophie said. "Why not? Everyone else does. Rand is the only one who—maybe—believes in me."

At Rand's name, Lotte lifted her head higher and began to pant harder. "I want to believe him when he says you won't hurt me," Sophie said. "It's just hard. Not your fault, I know. I think I used to like dogs before…before the accident." She ran her hand along the jaw, where the scars had been, before plastic surgery had rendered them invisible. "It was just so terrifying. I was only a child and it's like an involuntary reaction—I look at a dog and my body remembers."

Lotte sighed and rested her head on her paws, though her gold-brown eyes remained alert and fixed on Sophie. "If Rand and I are ever going to do anything about these feelings between us— whatever those feelings are—then you and I had better learn to get along." Sophie felt a little foolish, talking to the dog, but the conversation soothed her, and Lotte didn't seem to mind. And who else did she have to talk to about these things? "I've never been in love before," she said. "Not real love. So I don't know if this is what it feels like. And I don't even know if the two of us—together—are a good idea. I mean, I live in Madison. A long way from here. And he's here. And then there's Lauren. When they find her— and I have to believe they'll find her—I have no idea what she's been through. She may need me to focus all my attention on her, and would that be fair to Rand?"

Lotte lifted her head and whined.

"You're right," Sophie said. "It wouldn't be fair. So I shouldn't lead him on. I should just forget about him and go back to Madison when this is over and…" And what? Mope around with a broken heart? That sounded so melodramatic, but if leaving Rand behind didn't break her heart, she knew she'd at least be badly bruised. And for what? Not because she was so devoted to Madison, Wisconsin, and her job there. But because she was a coward. Afraid of getting hurt. Not just physically injured by Rand's dog, but emotionally wounded by his possible rejection. After all, she wasn't like Lauren. She wasn't beautiful and charming and she hadn't been born knowing how to captivate a guy. Sophie was quiet and plain and ordinary. No match for an edgy guy like Rand, with his tattoos and muscles and dangerous job. They weren't a bit alike and shouldn't a couple be at least a little compatible if they were going to build a long-term relationship?

"What do you think?" Sophie asked the dog. "Could Rand really love someone like me?"

Lotte leaped to her feet, every hair on her back standing on end. A deep growl made Sophie feel cold clear through, and when Lotte barked, Sophie screamed and stood on the sofa, looking wildly around for some weapon with which to defend herself.

Lotte rushed toward her, then past her. Weak-kneed and dry-mouthed, Sophie realized the dog was barking at the door. And not just barking, but jumping and pawing at the wood. Muffled voices sounded, their words indistinct.

"Who is it?" Sophie called, still standing on the sofa. "Who's out there?"

The door burst open, slamming hard against the wall. Lotte's barking grew more furious. Sophie was aware of two men rushing into the room. Then someone threw a blanket over her and wrapped strong arms around her. She struggled, kicking with her legs, her arms pinned. The dog's barking almost drowned out the men's shouting and her own muffled screams. A gunshot reverberated and then everything went black as she was dragged away.

MARCO REACHED LAUREN first and put a gloved hand over her mouth to stop her screaming. "It's all right," he said, his soft, deep voice soothing her. "We're here to rescue you."

She nodded, blue eyes wide in her pale face. Marco removed his hand. "Thank God," she said, her eyes wet with unshed tears. "I thought I'd never get out of here."

"You can tell us everything later," Rand said. "We've got to go before someone realizes the guards aren't reporting in." If Marco was right, the first guard had already missed his check-in period. Reinforcements might be on their way already.

Lauren climbed out of the bed and grabbed a robe—a long pink-and-gold brocade affair that looked like something out of a period movie. Something a queen or a movie star would wear. She shoved her feet into kitten-heeled slippers. Marco eyed them skeptically. "Don't you have anything sturdier?"

"Unfortunately, no. Richard won't let me have anything else."

"So, is he your boyfriend or something?" Rand asked.

Marco shot him a warning look and shook his head. But why not get the truth out in the open right away?

"My boyfriend?" Lauren laughed, a sound

like bells. "Please, no. Though if you ask him, he calls himself my fiancé. He's convinced if he keeps me here long enough I'll wear down and agree to marry him. He's sick, that's what he is." She sashed the robe tighter and tucked her hand into the crook of Marco's elbow. "Let's get out of here."

"We'll have to go back the way we came." Marco pointed to the door. "How often do the guards change?"

"They work six-hour shifts, I think," she said. "This one just came on a couple of hours ago." She gingerly stepped around the guard's prone figure. "I hope you hit him hard," she said to Marco, her tone conversational. "He was always trying to look down my gown and feel me up every chance he got." She shuddered. "A really foul man. I mean, at least Richard is a gentleman, even if he is delusional."

"We should move him out of the way," Rand said. "If someone comes along, maybe they'll think he deserted his post."

Marco grunted in agreement and grabbed the guard's ankles. Rand took his shoulders and they dragged him some distance to a side passage, the man glaring up at them malevolently the entire time. They left his weapons in a different side passage, then returned to Lauren, who waited at the entrance to her underground bedroom.

Rand studied her closely. He thought he saw some resemblance to Sophie, in the sharpness of her chin and the shape of her nose. But in demeanor the two sisters were nothing alike—Sophie quiet and serious, Lauren sparkling and chatty.

She must have felt his gaze on her. She looked over her shoulder at him and asked, "How did you find me? I was giving up hope."

"Your sister," he said. "Sophie traveled here from Wisconsin and demanded we keep looking for you. She refused to give up."

Tears glistened in her eyes once more. "Sophie has never given up on me," she said.

"Are you doing okay?" Marco asked. "Do you need anything before we head out?"

"I'm fine." Her smile dazzled. Even Marco looked dazed by it. "Richard makes sure I have all my medications. He denies me nothing, except my freedom."

He nodded and took her arm. "Let's go, then."

But just as they prepared to turn into the passage leading toward the exit, they heard someone coming. "That will be the guard coming to check on me," Lauren whispered. "They do a bed check every hour. If I'm not there, they'll raise the alarm."

Marco turned her around and they hurried back to the chamber. "Quick, back under the covers," he said. "Let the guard see you're okay. Then we'll have an hour before the next check—provided they don't discover the missing guard."

"Where will you be?" she asked, crawling into the bed and pulling up the covers.

"Under the bed." He slid under one side, and Rand rolled under the other.

The guard shuffled into the room. "Good evening," Lauren greeted him brightly.

"You're supposed to be asleep," the guard said.

"I'm having trouble sleeping. I sent the other guard to the house to get me my pills."

"He's not supposed to leave you unguarded," he said.

"Oh, it'll be all right. Who's going to find me down here?"

The guard grunted. "It's just as well you're awake. We brought you some company."

"Company?" Lauren sounded puzzled.

"She says she's your sister." Rand, watching from beneath the bed, stared in horror as a second man entered the room, dragging a bound-and-gagged Sophie behind him.

"You two can have a little reunion," the first guard said, and pushed Sophie onto the bed beside Lauren. Then the men left.

As soon as the guards were gone, Rand and Marco rolled from beneath the bed. Lauren was already kneeling beside her sister, struggling with her bonds.

Rand stripped off the tape over Sophie's mouth while Marco cut the ties on her wrists. "Lauren!" she cried, hugging her sister close.

The two women cried and exclaimed, until Marco finally interrupted. "We have to get out of here," he said.

"Are you all right?" Rand put an arm around Sophie, feeling her tremble. "Did they hurt you?"

She shook her head, but tears streamed down her cheeks. "But I'm afraid they shot Lotte. She did what you said she would do. She tried to protect me. But they had guns…"

His chest constricted as he thought of the dog, but he shoved the emotions aside. He had to focus on the situation at hand, on Sophie and Lauren and helping them escape.

They started back the way they had come, but skidded to a stop when they spotted not one, but two guards in the passage ahead. "Is there another way out?" Marco asked.

"There's the passage to the house," Lauren said. "There's no guard there, since the only place it goes is the house."

"Let's go," Rand said. "Once there, we can steal a vehicle and get away faster."

They rushed along the passage Lauren indicated, sacrificing stealth for speed. But one of the guards must have heard them and sounded the alarm. Marco grabbed Lauren's hand and pulled her forward. "Faster!" he commanded.

Sophie grasped Rand's hand and they hurried to keep up, but Lauren and Marco were faster and the two couples soon became separated. "Which way did they go?" Sophie asked.

Rand stopped and studied the dust at their feet. In the dark passageway it was impossible to make out distinct footprints. "Marco!" he shouted.

But the only answer was a deafening explosion that knocked him off his feet, and a shower of boulders crashed down around them.

Chapter Sixteen

Sophie came to, aching and disoriented in the darkness, choking in the dust. She closed her eyes and rested her head against the stone floor, willing memory to return. Back at Rand's duplex, after she'd been wrapped in the blanket, someone had stuffed her into the backseat of a vehicle while a second person bound her wrists and ankles. They'd driven for some time, then bumped down a rough road. Her captors cut the ties at her ankles so that she could walk, but gagged her and kept her wrapped in the blanket until she stood outside the passage that led to Sophie's room.

Tears streamed down her face as she remembered the shock and delight of seeing her sister at last, and Rand there with her.

Rand! Where was he? She felt all around her in the darkness until she encountered cloth, hard muscle and bone beneath. "Rand!" She curled her fingers around whatever part of the body she held. "Rand, please tell me you're all right."

"Sophie?" He tried to sit up, then fell back, moaning. She felt her way up his body to his head and caressed his face with her hands, then kissed his cheek. "Rand, wake up," she pleaded.

"I'm awake." His voice sounded strained.

"Are you all right?" she asked. "Are you hurt?"

"I got a bump on the head, but I'm okay." He levered himself up on his elbow. "I'm going to roll over. You reach into my pack and get a light so we can see our situation better."

"Okay."

He rolled onto his side and she sat up and felt in the outer pocket of his pack for the mini Maglite he told her she'd find there. When she switched it on she had to look away at first, it was so bright.

She handed the light to Rand and he sat up and shone it around them. They were in one end of a chamber blasted from the rock, the entrance and the other end of the space filled with fallen rock. "What happened?" she asked.

"Maybe the guards set off some kind of charge to collapse the tunnels." He continued to shine the light on the tumble of rock. "Maybe that was the plan."

"You mean Prentice would rather kill Lauren than let her escape?" It sounded like something out of a horror movie or something.

"If she's dead, she can't testify against him," Rand said. "And if she's buried in an old mine, the chances of us finding her are slim to none."

She choked back a sob. "Lauren can't be dead," she said. "Not when we've only just found her."

He gripped her arm. "Don't give up hope yet," he said. "We made it okay. And she's with Marco. He'll look after her."

She clutched his hand, trying to hang on to some of his calm, as well. "What do we do now?" she asked.

He slipped off his pack and pulled his radio from the belt at his side. "It's too far underground to transmit," he said, "but maybe headquarters can get a ping. They'll realize something has happened and come looking. Meanwhile, let's see if we can find a way out of here."

Together, they moved to the rubble-filled end of the chamber. He used the light to inspect every crevice between the rocks, but none revealed open space beyond. Sophie clawed at the rocks, trying to dislodge them. Maybe they could dig their way out—

Rand put a hand on her arm. "Stop. You're going to hurt yourself." He led her to the other side of the passage and spread his jacket for them to sit on. "The best thing to do is rest and wait."

"Wait for what?" she asked.

"Rescue. Someone will come for us, I'm sure."

"How can you be sure?"

"You heard the captain. We're all in this together. A team. You don't leave a team member behind."

She wanted to believe him, but she had no experience with that kind of loyalty. For so much of her life she and Lauren had only had each other. And Sophie was the dependable one, the sister who almost always came to the rescue. Except that now she was helpless to rescue Lauren, or herself.

"I can't believe Prentice was keeping Lauren prisoner down here," she said. "Why? It's not as if he could expect a big ransom for her or anything."

"Apparently he believed he could make her marry him if he kept her long enough," Rand said.

"But that's insane. And he looks so...so ordinary."

"I guess some sick minds can live under ordinary exteriors. But according to her he didn't mistreat her—he just wouldn't let her leave."

"She looked the same as always. Beautiful."

"I prefer the darker, quieter ones." Rand took her hand and squeezed it.

She smiled, even though he probably couldn't see it in the dark. She knew she wasn't beautiful like Lauren, but Rand made her feel beautiful. Special. She leaned against him, her hand wrapped in his. "If this had to happen, I'm glad I'm with you," she said.

"It's kind of nice to have some time alone with you." He smoothed his hand along her shoulder. "Not exactly the most romantic setting, though."

"I don't know about that." She snuggled closer. "It's dark. And private." He'd propped the flashlight against the rocks so that it cast an indirect golden glow, like a wall sconce, giving just enough light for her to make out his form, without a lot of details.

He turned his face toward hers and she kissed him. What she'd meant as a brief buss transformed into a long, lingering caress—contact that said all the things she could find no words for.

He cradled her face in both hands. "I've never met anyone like you," he said.

"You mean stubborn and afraid and crazy?" She tried to laugh, but the sound came out too shaky, revealing how important his answer was to her.

"I mean determined and brave and loyal. Amazing." He drew her to him in a deep, breath-stealing kiss, his hands sliding down her arms, then up her sides to cup her breasts, which felt swollen and heated at his touch.

She opened her mouth in a gasp and he swallowed the sound, his tongue sweeping over her lips, teasing into her mouth, enticing and erotic. She arched to him, wanting to be closer. Wanting more.

He slid his mouth from hers, and pressed his lips to her temple. "Maybe we should stop now," he said, his voice ragged.

Everything about this was wrong—the location, the timing, their clothes. Making love to Rand had felt inevitable for a while now, but she'd imagined candlelight and crisp sheets, soft music and silk, not rock walls and dirt floors, dusty jeans and dried blood. But being with him was the only good thing she had to hold on to now. Denying each other the one thing they wanted most seemed stupid. They might not have much time left; they might as well use that time for something good.

She unbuttoned the top button of his uniform shirt, resisting the urge to tear it from him. "I want this," she said. "More than I've ever wanted anything."

"I want it, too." He caressed her shoulders. "But you deserve better than this."

"Shhh." She pressed her lips to the triangle of exposed chest her unbuttoning had revealed. He tasted of sweat and dust. "This isn't about what either of us deserves."

He pulled her tight against him and kissed her, a hard, bruising kiss full of longing and regret. She cradled his head in her hands and opened her mouth to him, tangling her tongue with his, letting her need for him fill her and drive out the fear.

He slid both hands beneath her shirt, skimming along her ribs, then pushing her bra out of the way to cup her breasts, squeezing gently. The ridge of his erection pressed against her stomach; she could feel the heat even through the layers of cloth separating them. She reached down and rubbed her hand along the evidence of his desire, eliciting a groan of frustration from him.

He grasped her arms and held them over her head, then tugged off her shirt and bra, leaving her naked from the waist up. Goose bumps formed along her flesh, and she automatically tried to cover herself, but he kept hold of her arms, pulling them away. "You are so beautiful," he said, and bent to kiss the top of one breast, then the other.

She gasped when he drew her nipple into his mouth, the suction pulling between her legs. "Rand," she breathed, but he only suckled harder, leaving her light-headed and trembling.

He lowered the zipper of her jeans and slid his hand in to cup her over her underwear. She fumbled the rest of his shirt buttons loose and pushed the fabric away from his chest, then stilled, staring at what the parted fabric revealed.

He stilled also, and lifted his head, his eyes meeting hers. "I got my first tat when I was nineteen," he said. "I've been adding on ever since."

With one finger, she traced the lines of black ink: mountains and waves following the contours of his muscles, trees and rocks and animals inscribed across his torso and chest in an intricate mural. "It's beautiful," she said. "But not what I expected."

"I'm just full of surprises." He unbuckled his belt. "I can't wait to show you more."

They helped each other out of their clothes, even that mundane activity made sensual by the thrill of hands touching places they hadn't allowed themselves to touch before, revealing flesh they had never seen before. He made a pallet of their clothes on the floor and urged her down beside him. Side by side, they traced the contours of each other's bodies, exploring each peak and valley, discovering a map that was uniquely theirs. He learned she had had an appendectomy when she was twenty-four, and he had fallen while climbing a mountain at nineteen, leaving a jagged scar as a permanent reminder of that adventure.

He surprised her by stopping at one point and retrieving a condom from his pack. "It's not what you think," he said. "They make great temporary canteens."

She laughed. "Sure they do." She lay back and beckoned to him. "I don't care why you have one, just that you have one."

He kneeled beside her and ripped open the package, then sheathed himself. She held her breath as she watched him, her whole body tensed with need for him. When he positioned himself between her legs, she arched to him, all shyness vanished. "Hurry," she whispered.

She was more than ready for him, and the sensation of him filling her almost sent her over the edge. She tightened around him and he shaped his hands to her buttocks and pulled her even closer. "Look at me," he said.

She stared into his eyes, and the grimness of their surroundings, the rock and sand and darkness, receded. She lost herself in those intense brown eyes, and in the waves of desire buffeting her with each powerful thrust of his body. His hands caressed as his body moved, the need within her coiling tighter and tighter. "Don't hold back," he urged, so she didn't, and her climax rocketed through her, stripping away the last fragment of fear and hesitation that had bound her.

She clung to him, stroking his back, his chest, leaning forward to trace her tongue along the line of a tattooed mountain range. As she dragged her tongue across the flat brown nipple half-hidden in the lines of the artwork, he cried out his own release and convulsed against her. She held him tightly, eyes closed, listening to the strong, steady rhythm of his heartbeat, bringing them back to themselves.

They lay in each other's arms, their discarded clothes drawn around them as makeshift bedding. "Is it all right if I switch off the flashlight?" he asked. "We need to save the batteries."

"All right." She closed her own eyes, but even that didn't shut out the depth of the darkness when he switched off the little light. Only the solid feel of his chest against the side of her face, and the hard muscle of his arms pulling her to him, kept her grounded. "What do we do now?" she asked.

"I don't know. I only had the one condom."

She laughed, something she would never have thought she could do, considering the circumstances. "That's disappointing news," she said. "But I meant, what are we going to do about getting out of here?"

"I don't know yet, but we'll figure something out. For now, we need to sleep. We'll think better when we're rested."

"All right." She lay still, sure she'd never be able to relax, but gradually sleep did steal over her. In the security of Rand's arms, she relaxed. Later, they'd think of something. They didn't have any choice.

SOPHIE WOKE TO A LOW, groaning noise, like some ancient animal moving in the depths of the cavern. "Rand!" She shook him, hard. "Rand, wake up!"

He shifted beneath her, sitting up, his arm still around her, pulling her up with him. "What is it?" he asked, his voice only a little groggy.

"That noise. What is it?"

They listened, and it came again, a long, low moan, primitive and chilling. Rand switched on the light and began sorting through their clothes. "Get dressed," he said. "Hurry."

She pulled on underwear and pants and reached for her shirt. "What is it?" she asked, his anxious expression feeding her own fear. "Is it some kind of animal?"

"No animal." He buttoned his shirt halfway, then pulled on his pack. "It's the tunnels. Timbers shifting."

"The tunnels? I don't understand." She sat and began pulling on her shoes.

"We need to shelter along the wall, where the rock is thickest." He pulled her to her feet. "I think we might be in for another cave-in."

Chapter Seventeen

Sophie buried her face against Rand's chest and put her hands over her ears, trying to block out the groan of splintering timbers and crash of falling rock. Only his arms holding her tightly kept the panic at bay. With Rand, she could be strong enough to get through this.

Eerie silence settled over them. "What happened?" she asked. "Did they set off another charge?"

"I don't think so," he said. "I think the timbers will shift and settle for a while after an explosion. It's one of the things that make mine rescue work so dangerous." He coughed and switched on his flashlight. "Hey, take a look at this!"

She didn't want to look, didn't want to see their world reduced even further to a rocked-in tomb. But something in his voice encouraged her to lift her head and peer down the narrow beam of light.

Rather than reducing their world, this latest

collapse had opened the way into a new passage. "Is that a light up ahead?" she asked.

"Let's go find out." He took her hand and helped her over the rubble. In a few moments, they stood on the other side of the debris, in a smooth-walled tunnel. "Why does this section look different?" she asked.

"I think this must be the passage leading to the house." He ran his hand over the pale surface of the wall on their right. "It's poured concrete," he said. "Like one of those big highway culverts." He drew his gun. "Stay behind me. In case we run into one of Prentice's guards."

But they met no one in the tunnel, and no one waited at the door at the end. Rand tried the knob, but it wouldn't turn. "Stand back," he told her.

She took two steps back and covered her ears, expecting he'd shoot off the lock, as she'd seen in movies. Instead, he slammed his heel into the lock, collapsing it inward. The door swung open. They waited, but no one emerged. No one shouted. No alarms sounded.

Rand motioned her forward and cautiously, they stepped into what appeared at first to be a closet. He shone the light around the paneled walls until the beam illuminated a steel door.

"It's an elevator," Sophie said.

"Looks like it." He pressed the single lighted

button on the wall, and the door slid open. They stepped inside and Rand pressed the number *one*. After a few seconds, the doors silently closed and the car began to rise.

The elevator opened and they faced another door, this one unlocked, and it opened into a coat closet on the mansion's first floor. They passed through the closet, into the deserted front hall of Richard Prentice's mansion. "Where is everyone?" Sophie whispered.

"I hear something down there." Rand motioned with the pistol toward the back of the house. As they walked closer, she could hear a whirring sound and see the light spilling into the corridor.

Richard Prentice stood beside a filing cabinet, pulling out papers, a handful at a time, and depositing them in a whirring shredder. He looked up at their approach and frowned. "I don't have time to talk now, Officer," he said. "I'm very busy."

Rand motioned for Sophie to step back, then addressed the billionaire. "Richard Prentice, you're under arrest for the kidnapping of Lauren Starling."

Prentice inserted another sheaf of papers into the shredder, and raised his voice to be heard over the whirring. "I wouldn't believe anything poor Lauren tells you," he said. "She's crazy, you know. Completely unbalanced."

"Lauren is not crazy." Sophie couldn't keep quiet any longer. If anyone here was unbalanced, it was Richard Prentice. "She certainly didn't lock herself in that mine all these weeks," she said.

Prentice shook his head. "Lauren suffers from severe paranoia. She believed people were trying to kill her. I suppose she's transferred those feelings to me now. She came to me and I tried to help her. I care about her and I thought with time and attention, she'd recover. I see that's impossible now."

He sounded so calm and reasonable. So sane. If she hadn't known better, even Sophie might have believed him. "You were holding her prisoner in a mine," she protested.

"I created that room in the mine to reassure her." He continued shredding documents as he spoke. "She felt safe and protected there, at least at first."

"Liar," Sophie said. "Don't think your money will protect you now."

"You need to come with me, sir," Rand said. "You have the right to remain silent—"

Sophie didn't see the gun in Prentice's hands until it fired. She screamed as Rand fired his own weapon, but Prentice was already racing toward a door on the other side of the room. Rand shoved Sophie to the floor and fired again, bullets striking the door frame as Prentice jerked it open and threw himself outside.

Rand raced after him, Sophie trailing after. When she burst through the door she spotted a waiting helicopter, Richard Prentice running toward its open door.

"He's getting away!" she shouted as the door to the helicopter slammed shut, and the aircraft rose into a sky streaked pink with the dawn.

A black-and-white Ranger Brigade vehicle raced into the yard and skidded to a halt near where the helicopter had waited. Michael and Graham climbed out of the front seat, while Marco and Lauren exited the back. No longer the elegant newscaster who had smiled from television screens and billboards, Lauren's face was streaked with dirt, her hair long and limp, a sweatshirt and pants hanging on her small frame. But at the sight of her sister, she broke into a smile. "Sophie!" she cried, and held out her arms.

Sophie didn't try to hold back the tears as she embraced Lauren. "I've been so worried about you," she said. "What happened?"

"Marco and I escaped during the explosion," she said. "He found a way out of the mine.

Then we went for help. But I was so worried about you."

"I'm fine. But Richard Prentice got away." She looked up, toward the fast-departing silhouette of the helicopter.

"We'll find him," Graham's expression was grim, but determined. "We have more than enough evidence now to charge him with a long list of crimes, thanks to Ms. Starling."

"His lawyers won't pull him out of the fire this time," Rand said. "We'll make sure of that."

Sophie clung tightly to her sister's hand and watched the helicopter until it disappeared over a distant mountain. She wanted to believe justice would be served, and Richard Prentice would be punished for what he'd done, but the memory of him standing before the shredder, explaining away every bit of evidence against him with the assurance of a man who can buy the best lawyers and the best reputation, made her sick to her stomach. Maybe no matter how hard they all tried, he was a man who was truly above the law.

THE DAY AFTER her dramatic rescue, dressed in a new suit, her hair carefully styled and makeup perfected, Lauren Starling stood before two dozen reporters at the Dragon Point overlook in Black Canyon of the Gunnison National Park. Flanked by Captain Graham Ellison and Agent

Marco Cruz of The Ranger Brigade, she looked composed and professional, and much calmer than Sophie would have been in her position.

Sophie waited with Rand to one side of the gathering, marveling at her sister's composure. "I want to thank The Ranger Brigade for their tireless efforts to locate and rescue me," Lauren said, in the smooth, modulated tones of a professional broadcaster. "And I especially want to thank my sister, Sophie Montgomery, who put aside everything to come to my aid in my time of need. People talk about the depths of brotherly love, but nothing can match the depths of a sister's devotion." She smiled at Sophie, and dozens of cameras flashed.

Lauren directed that dazzling smile to the reporters in front of her. "And now I'll take a few questions."

"Ms. Starling, what do you say to Richard Prentice's assertion that everything you've told us today is a lie, an elaborate scenario that resulted from your own mental illness?" The reporter, a man in a bow tie whom Sophie didn't recognize, hurled the question like a dagger.

Lauren's smile vanished. Maybe Sophie was the only one who saw the flash of pain in her eyes, the tightening of her fingers on the edge of the podium, the tension in her shoulders. She quickly masked the fear, and replaced it with a stern, but determined look. "Mr. Prentice is facing many years in prison for his crimes, and the complete ruin of his reputation," she said evenly. "He is desperate to blame anyone but himself for his misdeeds. He is the one who is lying."

"But you are mentally ill," the reporter persisted. "You've admitted to a diagnosis of bipolar disorder."

"Yes, I suffer from an illness shared by five-point-seven million people in this country alone," she said. "And as with other illnesses, such as diabetes or asthma, I take medication and have adjusted my lifestyle to control the disease. I was definitely in my right mind when Richard Prentice kidnapped me and held me hostage for six weeks. He's the one who's delusional, if he thinks he can dismiss that behavior as a product of my imagination."

"In the statement he issued this morning, Mr. Prentice says the Rangers have no proof of the other charges against him," another reporter read from a tablet computer. "He says, quote, 'The Ranger Brigade continue their established pattern of harassment and character assassination with these unfounded claims. I have no connection to drug dealers, murders, smuggling and the other crimes they have charged me with.' End quote. What do you say to that?"

"I came to Montrose to interview a witness

and obtain photographic proof of Mr. Prentice's ties to drug dealing in the area," she said. "That witness has since been murdered, and Mr. Prentice tried to silence me, but failed. Once he is returned for trial, the world will see we have plenty of proof."

"If he wanted to silence you, why didn't he just kill you?" a female reporter asked.

"That will be explained in the trial." Graham stepped forward. The Rangers' attorney had advised Lauren not to go into Prentice's plan to persuade her to marry him. The scheme was outlandish enough that some in the media might latch on to it as proof of Prentice's claims that Lauren was delusional. After all, the stoic billionaire didn't strike people as the type to obsess over a woman, no matter how beautiful.

"That's all the questions we have time for today," Graham said, and reporters immediately turned their attention to him, firing questions about the Rangers' case against Richard Prentice. Lauren moved to stand beside Marco Cruz. Sophie had noticed her sister seemed to feel safest near the handsome, taciturn officer.

The press conference ended and the reporters and cameramen began to move back toward their cars. But one man, tall and blond and dressed in slacks and a dress shirt, the sleeves carefully folded back to reveal muscular forearms, broke away from the crowd and moved toward Lauren. "Phil!" she said, her expression wary. "I didn't expect to see you here."

He glanced at the officers flanking her and held out his hands, palms up. "I'm not here to cause trouble. I just wanted to say I'm glad you're okay. Despite what other people might think—" again, a look at the officers "—I didn't have anything to do with what happened to you."

"I know you didn't." Lauren's smile would have melted chocolate. "Take care of yourself, Phil."

"I'm trying." He adjusted his collar. "I'm checking into a rehab program in Grand Junction this afternoon."

"That's a good idea," Lauren said.

"Yeah, well, I guess this is goodbye. For now, anyway."

"Goodbye, Phil." Marco took her arm and she turned away, toward his waiting car.

"She did great," Sophie whispered to Rand. "She's so brave."

He took her hand and squeezed it. "You're the one who's brave. I'm proud of you."

She had to look away from the admiration in his eyes, aware of the people crowded around them. Her gaze focused on the dog beside him. "I'm glad Lotte's all right," she said. "I was worried."

"Lucky those guys were terrible shots." Rand

scratched the dog behind the ears. Then he put his arm around Sophie. "Let's go for a walk."

He led her down the path to the very edge of the canyon, where she looked out at the figures of the fighting dragons etched in the opposite wall of the chasm. Though composed by nature, they looked like Chinese paintings, the giant figures in red and black crisp against the gray stone walls.

"What will you do now that Lauren is safe?" he asked.

"I don't know. I'm thinking of staying here for a while, to make sure she's all right." Though Lauren hadn't said much about her ordeal, Sophie sensed her sister was still fragile. She'd need support for the long trial—both in the media and in the courtroom—that lay ahead. "I don't really have anything to go back to in Wisconsin. My job stopped challenging me a long time ago, and I could probably find another one here."

"Does that mean you'll stay in Montrose?"

"I'm thinking about it. Lauren plans to stay here. She'll do all she can to see that Richard Prentice is convicted. It's not going to be easy for her. I want to be here to help."

"I'd like it if you stayed."

She met his eyes, searching for the emotions behind his words. Did he mean he'd like it if they got to know each other better, maybe casually dated? Or did he want what she wanted, to continue this deeper connection she felt for him? "Why would you like me to stay?" she asked.

He smoothed his palm down her arm, then caught her hand in his. "I used to joke that Lotte was the only woman I needed in my life," he said. "But I was wrong. I need you. I think I've stayed single until now because I was waiting for you."

"I can't make any promises right now," she said. "Not while things are still so unsettled for Lauren."

"Just say you'll give me a chance—you'll give us a chance." He squeezed her hand.

She squeezed back. "Yes. I want that." She wanted Rand in her life—for a long time to come. Maybe even forever.

Lotte whined. They looked at the dog. "What about Lotte?" he asked. "The two of us are a package deal."

"I've never felt this way about anyone else." She swallowed, her mouth suddenly dry. "I love you, Rand. It scares me a little."

"I love you, too. And we both know you're not going to a let a little fear stop you."

They kissed, a light, brief contact that held the promise of much more. Later, when they were alone.

Lotte whined again, a soft, pleading sound.

Sophie put out her hand and stroked the dog's soft head, trembling only a little as she did so. "I'm learning to love Lotte, too," she said. "She risked her life to try to save me. And since she's so important to you, I want her to be important to me, too."

He put his hand over hers and they stood that way for a long moment, man, woman and dog. An unlikely circle of love. Sophie sighed with happiness. She had spent so many years being afraid, when all along she'd had the power— the courage—inside her to save herself. To find the love she deserved, with a man who was truly worthy.

* * * * *

Cindi Myers's THE RANGER BRIGADE *miniseries concludes next month.
You can find* BLACK CANYON CONSPIRACY *wherever Harlequin Intrigue books and ebooks are sold!*

Read on for a sneak peek of
LONE RIDER
The next installment in
THE MONTANA HAMILTONS *series*
from New York Times *bestselling author*
B.J. Daniels.
When danger claims her, rescue comes from
the one man she least expects...

CHAPTER ONE

THE MOMENT JACE CALDER saw his sister's face, he feared the worst. His heart sank. Emily, his troubled little sister, had been doing so well since she'd gotten the job at the Sarah Hamilton Foundation in Big Timber, Montana.

"What's wrong?" he asked as he removed his Stetson, pulled up a chair at the Big Timber Java coffee shop and sat down across from her. Tossing his hat on the seat of an adjacent chair, he braced himself for bad news.

Emily blinked her big blue eyes. Even though she was closing in on twenty-five, he often caught glimpses of the girl she'd been. Her pixie cut, once a dark brown like his own hair, was dyed black. From thirteen on, she'd been piercing anything she could. At sixteen she'd begun getting tattoos and drinking. It wasn't until she'd turned seventeen that she'd run away, taken up with a thirty-year-old biker drug-dealer thief and ended up in jail for the first time.

But while Emily still had the tattoos and the piercings, she'd changed after the birth of her daughter, and after snagging this job with Bo Hamilton.

"What's wrong is Bo," his sister said. Bo had insisted her employees at the foundation call her by her first name. "Pretty cool for a boss, huh?" his sister had said at the time. He'd been surprised. That didn't sound like the woman he knew.

But who knew what was in Bo's head lately. Four months ago her mother, Sarah, who everyone believed dead the past twenty-two years, had suddenly shown up out of nowhere. According to what he'd read in the papers, Sarah had no memory of the past twenty-two years.

He'd been worried it would hurt the foundation named for her. Not to mention what a shock it must have been for Bo.

Emily leaned toward him and whispered, "Bo's… She's gone."

"Gone?"

"Before she left Friday, she told me that she would be back by ten this morning. She hasn't shown up, and no one knows where she is."

That *did* sound like the Bo Hamilton he knew. The thought of her kicked up that old ache inside him. He'd been glad when Emily had found a job and moved back to town with her baby girl.

But he'd often wished her employer had been anyone but Bo Hamilton—the woman he'd once asked to marry him.

He'd spent the past five years avoiding Bo, which wasn't easy in a county as small as Sweet Grass. Crossing paths with her, even after five years, still hurt. It riled him in a way that only made him mad at himself for letting her get to him after all this time.

"What do you mean, *gone*?" he asked now.

Emily looked pained. "I probably shouldn't be telling you this—"

"Em," he said impatiently. She'd been doing so well at this job, and she'd really turned her life around. He couldn't bear the thought that Bo's disappearance might derail her second chance. Em's three-year-old daughter, Jodie, desperately needed her mom to stay on track.

Leaning closer again, she whispered, "Apparently there are funds missing from the foundation. An auditor's been going over all the records since Friday."

He sat back in surprise. No matter what he thought of Bo, he'd never imagined this. The woman was already rich. She wouldn't need to divert funds...

"And that's not the worst of it," Emily said. "I was told she's on a camping trip in the mountains."

"So, she isn't really gone."

Em waved a hand. "She took her camping gear, saddled up and left Saturday afternoon. Apparently she's the one who called the auditor, so she knew he would be finished and wanting to talk to her this morning!"

Jace considered this news. If Bo really were on the run with the money, wouldn't she take her passport and her SUV as far as the nearest airport? But why would she run at all? He doubted Bo had ever had a problem that her daddy, the senator, hadn't fixed for her. She'd always had a safety net. Unlike him.

He'd been on his own since eighteen. He'd been a senior in high school, struggling to pay the bills, hang on to the ranch and raise his wild kid sister after his parents had been killed in a small plane crash. He'd managed to save the ranch, but he hadn't been equipped to raise Emily and had made his share of mistakes.

A few months ago, his sister had got out of jail and gone to work for Bo. He'd been surprised she'd given Emily a chance. He'd had to readjust his opinion of Bo—but only a little. Now this.

"There has to be an explanation," he said, even though he knew firsthand that Bo often acted impulsively. She did whatever she wanted, damn the world. But now his little sister was part of that world. How could she leave Emily and the rest of the staff at the foundation to face this alone?

"I sure hope everything is all right," his sister said. "Bo is so sweet."

Sweet wasn't a word he would have used to describe her. Sexy in a cowgirl way, yes, since most of the time she dressed in jeans, boots and a Western shirt—all of which accented her very nice curves. Her long, sandy-blond hair was often pulled up in a ponytail or wrestled into a braid that hung over one shoulder. Since her wide green eyes didn't need makeup to give her that girl-next-door look, she seldom wore it.

"I can't believe she wouldn't show up. Something must have happened," Emily said loyally.

He couldn't help being skeptical based on Bo's history. But given Em's concern, he didn't want to add his own kindling to the fire.

"Jace, I just have this bad feeling. You're the best tracker in these parts. I know it's a lot to ask, but would you go find her?"

He almost laughed. Given the bad blood between him and Bo? "I'm the last person—"

"I'm really worried about her. I know she wouldn't run off."

Jace wished *he* knew that. "Look, if you're really that concerned, maybe you should call the sheriff. He can get search and rescue—"

"No," Emily cried. "No one knows what's

going on over at the foundation. We have to keep this quiet. That's why you have to go."

He'd never been able to deny his little sister anything, but this was asking too much.

"Please, Jace."

He swore silently. Maybe he'd get lucky and Bo would return before he even got saddled up. "If you're that worried…" He got to his feet and reached for his hat, telling himself it shouldn't take him long to find Bo if she'd gone up into the Crazies, as the Crazy Mountains were known locally. He'd grown up in those mountains. His father had been an avid hunter who'd taught him everything about mountain survival.

If Bo had gone rogue with the foundation's funds… He hated to think what that would do not only to Emily's job but also to her recovery. She idolized her boss. So did Josie, who was allowed the run of the foundation office.

But finding Bo was one thing. Bringing her back to face the music might be another. He started to say as much to Emily, but she cut him off.

"Oh, Jace, thank you so much. If anyone can find her, it's you."

He smiled at his sister as he set his Stetson firmly on his head and made her a promise. "I'll find Bo Hamilton and bring her back." One way or the other.

CHAPTER TWO

BO HAMILTON ROSE with the sun, packed up camp and saddled up as a squirrel chattered at her from a nearby pine tree. Overhead, high in the Crazy Mountains, Montana's big, cloudless early summer sky had turned a brilliant blue. The day was already warm. Before she'd left, she'd heard a storm was coming in, but she'd known she'd be out of the mountains long before it hit.

She'd had a devil of a time getting to sleep last night, and after tossing and turning for hours in her sleeping bag, she had finally fallen into a death-like sleep.

But this morning, she'd awakened ready to face whatever would be awaiting her tomorrow back at the office in town. Coming up here in the mountains had been the best thing she could have done. For months she'd been worried and confused as small amounts of money kept disappearing from the foundation.

Then last week, she'd realized that more than a hundred thousand dollars was gone. She'd been so shocked that she hadn't been able to breathe, let alone think. That's when she'd called in an independent auditor. She just hoped she could find out what had happened to the money before anyone got wind of it—especially her father, Senator Buckmaster Hamilton.

Her stomach roiled at the thought. He'd always been so proud of her for taking over the reins of the foundation that bore her mother's name. All her father needed was another scandal. He was running for the presidency of the United States, something he'd dreamed of for years. Now his daughter was about to go to jail for embezzlement. She could only imagine his disappointment in her—not to mention what it might do to the foundation.

She loved the work the foundation did, helping small businesses in their community. Her father had been worried that she couldn't handle the responsibility. She'd been determined to show him he was wrong. And show herself, as well. She'd grown up a lot in the past five years, and running the foundation had given her a sense of purpose she'd badly needed.

That's why she was anxious to find out the results of the audit now that her head was clear. The mountains always did that for her. Breathing in the fresh air now, she swung up in the saddle, spurred her horse and headed down the trail toward the ranch. She'd camped only a couple of hours back into the mountain, so she still had plenty of time, she thought as she rode. The last thing she wanted was to be late to meet with the auditor.

She'd known for some time that there were… *discrepancies* in foundation funds. A part of her had hoped that it was merely a mistake—that someone would realize he or she had made an error—so she wouldn't have to confront anyone about the slip.

Bo knew how naive that was, but she couldn't bear to think that one of her employees was behind the theft. Yes, her employees were a ragtag bunch. There was Albert Drum, a seventy-two-year-young former banker who worked with the recipients of the foundation loans. Emily Calder, twenty-four, took care of the website, research, communication and marketing. The only other employee was forty-eight-year-old widow Norma Branstetter, who was in charge of fund-raising.

Employees and board members reviewed the applications that came in for financial help. But Bo was the one responsible for the money that came and went through the foundation.

Unfortunately, she trusted her employees so much that she often let them run the place, including dealing with the financial end of things. She hadn't been paying close enough attention. How else could there be unexplained expenditures?

Her father had warned her about the people she hired, saying she had to be careful. But she loved giving jobs to those who desperately needed another chance. Her employees had become a second family to her.

Just the thought that one of her employees might be responsible made her sick to her stomach. True, she was a sucker for a hard-luck story. But she trusted the people she'd hired. The thought brought tears to her eyes. They all tried so hard and were so appreciative of their jobs. She refused to believe any one of them would steal from the foundation.

So what had happened to the missing funds?

She hadn't ridden far when her horse nickered and raised his head as if sniffing the wind. Spurring him forward, she continued through the dense trees. The pine boughs sighed in the breeze, releasing the smells of early summer in the mountains she'd grown up with. She loved the Crazy Mountains. She loved them especially at this time of year. They rose from the valley into high snow-capped peaks, the awe-inspiring range running for miles to the north like a mountainous island in a sea of grassy plains.

What she appreciated most about the Crazies

was that a person could get lost in them, she thought. A hunter had done just that last year.

She'd ridden down the ridge some distance, the sun moving across the sky over her head, before she caught the strong smell of smoke. This morning she'd put her campfire out using the creek water nearby. Too much of Montana burned every summer because of lightning storms and careless people, so she'd made sure her fire was extinguished before she'd left.

Now reining in, she spotted the source of the smoke. A small campfire burned below her in the dense trees of a protected gully. She stared down into the camp as smoke curled up. While it wasn't that unusual to stumble across a backpacker this deep in the Crazies, it *was* strange for a camp to be so far off the trail. Also, she didn't see anyone below her on the mountain near the fire. Had whoever camped there failed to put out the fire before leaving?

Bo hesitated, feeling torn because she didn't want to take the time to ride all the way down the mountain to the out-of-the-way camp. Nor did she want to ride into anyone's camp unless necessary.

But if the camper had failed to put out the fire, that was another story.

"Hello?" she called down the mountainside.

A hawk let out a cry overhead, momentarily startling her.

"Hello?" she called again, louder.

No answer. No sign of anyone in the camp.

Bo let out an aggravated sigh and spurred her horse. She had a long ride back and didn't need a detour. But she still had plenty of time if she hurried. As she made her way down into the ravine, she caught glimpses of the camp and the smoking campfire, but nothing else.

The hidden-away camp finally came into view below her. She could see that whoever had camped there hadn't made any effort at all to put out the fire. She looked for horseshoe tracks but saw only boot prints in the dust that led down to the camp.

A quiet seemed to fall over the mountainside. No hawk called out again from high above the trees. No squirrel chattered at her from a pine bough. Even the breeze seemed to have gone silent.

Bo felt a sudden chill as if the sun had gone down—an instant before the man appeared so suddenly from out of the dense darkness of the trees. He grabbed her, yanked her down from the saddle and clamped an arm around her as he shoved the dirty blade of a knife in her face.

"Well, look at you," he said hoarsely against

her ear. "Ain't you a sight for sore eyes? Guess it's my lucky day."

JACE HAD JUST knocked at the door when another truck drove up from the direction of the corrals. As Senator Buckmaster Hamilton himself opened the door, he looked past Jace's shoulder. Jace glanced back to see Cooper Barnett climb out of his truck and walk toward them.

Jace turned back around. "I'm Jace Calder," he said, holding out his hand as the senator's gaze shifted to him.

The senator frowned but shook his hand. "I know who you are. I'm just wondering what's got you on my doorstep so early in the morning."

"I'm here about your daughter Bo."

Buckmaster looked to Cooper. "Tell me you aren't here about my daughter Olivia."

Cooper laughed. "My pregnant bride is just fine, thanks."

The senator let out an exaggerated breath and turned his attention back to Jace. "What's this about—" But before he could finish, a tall, elegant blonde woman appeared at his side. Jace recognized Angelina Broadwater Hamilton, the senator's second wife. The rumors about her being kicked out of the house to make way for Buckmaster's first wife weren't true, it seemed.

She put a hand on Buckmaster's arm. "It's the

auditor calling from the foundation office. He's looking for Bo. She didn't show up for work today, and there seems to be a problem."

"That's why I'm here," Jace said.

"Me, too," Cooper said, sounding surprised.

"Come in, then," Buckmaster said, waving both men inside. Once he'd closed the big door behind them, he asked, "Now, what's this about Bo?"

"I was just talking to one of the wranglers," Cooper said, jumping in ahead of Jace. "Bo apparently left Saturday afternoon on horseback, saying she'd be back this morning, but she hasn't returned."

"That's what I heard, as well," Jace said, taking the opening. "I need to know where she might have gone."

Both Buckmaster and Cooper looked to him. "You sound as if you're planning to go after her," the senator said.

"I am."

"Why would you do that? I didn't think you two were seeing each other?" Cooper asked like the protective brother-in-law he was.

"We're not," Jace said.

"Wait a minute," the senator said. "You're the one who stood her up for the senior prom. I'll never forget it. My baby cried for weeks."

Jace nodded. "That would be me."

"But you've dated Bo more recently than senior prom," Buckmaster was saying.

"Five years ago," he said. "But that doesn't have anything to do with this. I have my reasons for wanting to see Bo come back. My sister works at the foundation."

"Why wouldn't Bo come back?" the senator demanded.

Behind him, Angelina made a disparaging sound. "Because there's money missing from the foundation along with your daughter." She looked at Jace. "You said your sister works down there?"

He smiled, seeing that she was clearly judgmental of the "kind of people" Bo had hired to work at the foundation. "My sister doesn't have access to any of the money, if that's what you're worried about." He turned to the senator again. "The auditor is down at the foundation office, trying to sort it out. Bo needs to be there. I thought you might have some idea where she might have gone in the mountains. I thought I'd go find her."

The senator looked to his son-in-law. Cooper shrugged.

"Cooper, you were told she planned to be back Sunday?" her father said. "She probably changed her mind or went too far, not realizing how long it would take her to get back. If she had an appointment today with an auditor, I'm sure she's on her way as we speak."

"Or she's hiding up there and doesn't want to be found," Angelina quipped from the couch. "If she took that money, she could be miles from here by now." She groaned. "It's always something with your girls, isn't it?"

"I highly doubt Bo has taken off with any foundation money," the senator said and shot his wife a disgruntled look. "Every minor problem isn't a major scandal," he said and sighed, clearly irritated with his wife.

When he and Bo had dated, she'd told him that her stepmother was always quick to blame her and her sisters no matter the situation. As far as Jace could tell, there was no love lost on either side.

"Maybe we should call the sheriff," Cooper said.

Angelina let out a cry. "That's all we need— more negative publicity. It will be bad enough when this gets out. But if search and rescue is called in and the sheriff has to go up there… For all we know, Bo could be meeting someone in those mountains."

Jace hadn't considered she might have an accomplice. "That's why I'm the best person to go after her."

"How do you figure that?" Cooper demanded, giving him a hard look.

"She already doesn't like me, and the feeling is mutual. Maybe you're right and she's hightailing it home as we speak," Jace said. "But whatever's going on with her, I'm going to find her and make sure she gets back."

"You sound pretty confident of that," the senator said sounding almost amused.

"I know these mountains, and I'm not a bad tracker. I'll find her. But that's big country. My search would go faster if I have some idea where she was headed when she left."

"There's a trail to the west of the ranch that connects with the Sweet Grass Creek trail," her father said.

Jace rubbed a hand over his jaw. "That trail forks not far up."

"She usually goes to the first camping spot before the fork," the senator said. "It's only a couple of hours back in. I'm sure she wouldn't go any farther than that. It's along Loco Creek."

"I know that spot," Jace said.

Cooper looked to his father-in-law. "You want me to get some men together and go search for her? That makes more sense than sending—"

Buckmaster shook his head and turned to Jace. "I remember your father. The two of you were volunteers on a search years ago. I was impressed with both of you. I'm putting my money on you finding her if she doesn't turn up on her own. I'll give you 'til sundown."

"Make it twenty-four hours. There's a storm coming so I plan to be back before it hits. If we're both not back by then, send in the cavalry," he said and with a tip of his hat, headed for the door.

Behind him, he heard Cooper say, "Sending him could be a mistake."

"The cowboy's mistake," Buckmaster said. "I know my daughter. She's on her way back, and she isn't going to like that young man tracking her down. Jace Calder is the one she almost married."

Find out what happens next in
LONE RIDER
by New York Times
bestselling author B.J. Daniels
available August 2015,
wherever HQN Books and ebooks are sold.
www.Harlequin.com

LARGER-PRINT BOOKS!

HARLEQUIN

Presents®

PASSION GUARANTEED SEDUCTION

GET 2 FREE LARGER-PRINT NOVELS PLUS 2 FREE GIFTS!

YES! Please send me 2 FREE LARGER-PRINT Harlequin Presents® novels and my 2 FREE gifts (gifts are worth about $10). After receiving them, if I don't wish to receive any more books, I can return the shipping statement marked "cancel." If I don't cancel, I will receive 6 brand-new novels every month and be billed just $5.30 per book in the U.S. or $5.74 per book in Canada. That's a saving of at least 12% off the cover price! It's quite a bargain! Shipping and handling is just 50¢ per book in the U.S. and 75¢ per book in Canada.* I understand that accepting the 2 free books and gifts places me under no obligation to buy anything. I can always return a shipment and cancel at any time. Even if I never buy another book, the two free books and gifts are mine to keep forever.

176/376 HDN GHVY

Name	(PLEASE PRINT)	
Address		Apt. #
City	State/Prov.	Zip/Postal Code

Signature (if under 18, a parent or guardian must sign)

Mail to the Reader Service:
IN U.S.A.: P.O. Box 1867, Buffalo, NY 14240-1867
IN CANADA: P.O. Box 609, Fort Erie, Ontario L2A 5X3

**Are you a subscriber to Harlequin Presents® books
and want to receive the larger-print edition?
Call 1-800-873-8635 today or visit us at www.ReaderService.com.**

* Terms and prices subject to change without notice. Prices do not include applicable taxes. Sales tax applicable in N.Y. Canadian residents will be charged applicable taxes. Offer not valid in Quebec. This offer is limited to one order per household. Not valid for current subscribers to Harlequin Presents Larger-Print books. All orders subject to credit approval. Credit or debit balances in a customer's account(s) may be offset by any other outstanding balance owed by or to the customer. Please allow 4 to 6 weeks for delivery. Offer available while quantities last.

Your Privacy—The Reader Service is committed to protecting your privacy. Our Privacy Policy is available online at www.ReaderService.com or upon request from the Reader Service.

We make a portion of our mailing list available to reputable third parties that offer products we believe may interest you. If you prefer that we not exchange your name with third parties, or if you wish to clarify or modify your communication preferences, please visit us at www.ReaderService.com/consumerschoice or write to us at Reader Service Preference Service, P.O. Box 9062, Buffalo, NY 14240-9062. Include your complete name and address.

HPLP15

LARGER-PRINT BOOKS!
GET 2 FREE LARGER-PRINT NOVELS PLUS
2 FREE GIFTS!

From the Heart, For the Heart

HRLP15

LARGER-PRINT BOOKS!
GET 2 FREE LARGER-PRINT NOVELS PLUS
2 FREE GIFTS!

HARLEQUIN®

super romance®

More Story...More Romance

M POW